Sugartown

A collection of short stories and poems

Cat
Cochrane

ISBN: 9798354789993
ebook: available at amazon.co.uk

Book cover design by Andrew Taylor

Sugartown Contents

Dedicated to the McGougan Family
and my pal Suzie,
who
never
stopped
believing in me

Introduction

Between these pages are twelve short stories and thirteen poems. The common thread among them is Glasgow; its people, its spaces, its everyday events and its voice. Many of the tales are taken from snippets of life overheard in bus shelters, chippy queues, NHS waiting rooms...collectively the most daily routine of places.

Some are written in Glasgow vernacular, some aren't. Some are just a few pages long, most are longer. Some characters are amalgamations of real people, most are purely fictional, yet hopefully recognisable at the same time.

My aim is to entertain with the words and twists of these tales, at the same time dipping into the human condition that lives so richly in the Glaswegian sensibility. A Weegie is made up of many parts and indeed from many places outwith the city itself. As is often heard, *we're aw fae somewhere.*

Incidentally, the title is inspired by the city's abiding relationship with the sweet stuff—from the local merchants who capitalised on Caribbean slavery importing sugar to the banks of the River Clyde, to our love of sweeties and the contents of ginger bottles.

A big thanks to Andrew Taylor for his talent in designing the book's cover, to Marie Fleming for the edits and suggestions, to Maja Gerken for the fine-tooth combing and support...and to the people of Glasgow for their daily inspiration.

Coorie in, get comfy and enjoy a few wee reflections of a Dear Green Place...

The Hairdresser

I just kinda fell into the business of hair by accident really. It wasn't like I jumped headlong in. I used to be in a band. The Chow Mein Allstars. Stupid name altogether. When the phone rang with the hope of a potential booking, folk on the other end would ask for two Nasi Gorengs and a Kung Pao Chicken before you could set them right.

We'd started out as kids with a bunch of stretched elastic bands and a 1980s Casio keyboard. Reached the giddy heights of playing an engagement party at the Kirkintilloch Miners' Welfare too. We were really just a bunch of ruffians who acted like they'd been let loose on a shopping trolley half the time. I've always put our demise down to our singer, Julie, having a face that was better in soft focus and low saturation. A right scummy hue to her skin tone, ye know?

Anyway, when it all went inevitably tits the way up and *mea culpa* in my direction, I started seeing Johnny, a hair supplies salesman, as an act of *le* rebound. A barnet as slick as his patter, I kid you not. The number of times we had a quickie in the back of his Vauxhall Nova and I'd end up with a tin of Dax Wax stuck to my arse—I had to stop wearing cream linen slacks due to the grease. So Johnny had connections all over town with this salon and that. He won a hair stylist training voucher due to exceeding

1

half-year sales targets or some such tosh, giving it to me as a birthday present. I finished with him three weeks later.

I knew I was always good with my hands so it stood to reason that I made an impression on the course. *Chrissy Scissorhawns...* I still have the wee white label they gave me on the first day. I had this image of Rita Rusk and John Frieda and Lulu popping into me for a trim. All I can say is I'm glad *I* never paid for the course. It was more blue rinse and the want of a return of the poodle perm as soon as I laid eyes on. Still, I enjoyed being the star of the class and so started my journey on the pursuit of an unbeaten follicled path. Once I got the skill set up and a bit of experience, I tried to get back with Johnny...well I tried to get back with the easy access to his bulging hoard of semi and quasi-permanent tints in the boot of that Nova, but he'd went back to his wife in the meantime. For every Dax stain, if only I'd kept the tin.

I'll skip the years of slings and arrows and outrageous fortunes and fast forward to the hey presto. Looking back, I should've just stuck to the homers, but of course when word gets around that there's talent on the block, well they come-a-calling, don't they? It only started as a favour to big Ina, for days she'd go to the cash and carry or take her Billy to the cancer ward for his treatments. But Tuesday mornings and Friday afternoons soon turned into being taken a len ae, ye know? I wasn't best pleased to be working in an establishment by the name of *Curl Up and Dye*, but some things you can get away with in

Glasgow, and I suppose it stuck out in the *Yellow Pages*. Ina had her regulars, of course. Two Bob Annies the half of them, looking like geriatric Gummi Bears sitting there under the dryers, and always trying their brass necks for a freebie. "This is a business, no a charity," never seemed to phase them. Well of course, knowing me, I couldn't hold my tongue when the worst of the gang said, "Do you know you've got a right chip oan yer shoulder?" I replied, "You've got a right bouffant from 1984 sitting on both of yours, but we'll not split the proverbial hair about it."

When wee Billy went, Ina never picked up a pair of scissors again, and to be fair no one could blame her. Around this time, I was getting fed up with traipsing my gear on and off Glasgow buses to the homers, and as I'd failed my driving test for the fifth time, I took it as a sign I wasn't born to be the mobile sort. My own premises were clearly the future. The future was bright, the future was ginger...

You'd think getting the finance and dealing with builders and their idea of rip-off prices *vis-à-vis* fixtures and fittings would be the biggest challenge at the get-go. But that was a doddle, compared to finding the right staff. I mean, I like my wee trainee lassies to have a decent tongue in their head, so when I asked Lucy what's a polite word she'd use if she had to swear on impulse and she came away with *cunt,* I thought...(well, think the sound of a wrong answer on *Family Fortunes)*. Then there was big Hassan with a glowing reference from the Turkish crowd round the corner. Thought it was a coup landing Hassan as there were things he could do design-wise with a set of trimmers that would make Picasso seethe with envy. But it turned out he and his young Turks were inseparable, what with their carjacking and general riot running on the side. I nicknamed him Angry Barber and his 40 thieves.

Then there was Lena. She was a cracking stylist, but as daft as the top of that hair brush. Lena would come into work every other day, veins fizzed with liquor. Honest to God, she was so high half the time she walked around wearing a cloud for a hat. It came to the stage where she wasn't even safe around the alcohol kept for sterilising the combs, let alone a pair of scissors. Nice lassie, but she had me running about like an arse on a fly trying to calm her down.

That's when Dan Dan Corcoran came in to save the day. Big Dan had a right purposeful gait and an imposing frame that filled a doorway, ye know the sort. Way ahead of his time, he was doing a great horseshoe flat top while Vidal Sassoon was still scratching about on his haunches. When Dan dropped his scissors, I dropped my inhibitions, I'm telling you. Like an unstoppable force meets an immovable object, we were like the Liz Taylor and Richard Burton of the Glasgow hair fraternity. Who says you can't mix business with pleasure?

It's like I've always said, if only hairdressers and taxi drivers ran the country we'd get it moving and all have a funky barnet, to boot. But then that's why this nation is on the bones of its arse. I've always fancied doing the hair behind the scenes of one of they political conferences. I mean, I've no allegiances either way when it comes to voting hour, but would it not have been good telly if I'd sent Nicola Sturgeon onto *Question Time* sporting a right good set of cornrows, or that Ruth Davidson on with a poodle perm?

But I have had offers, of course, to do demos and parties. But some of those event coordinators are right up their own bahookies. When I say demonstrations, it was usually me that started them.

Once did the birthday bash of very famous ex-TV presenter. For 20-odd years no one ever knew she was under a wig. Jesus, I nearly collapsed. *Alopecia totalis*. Mind you, when I gave her big bush of a wig a good tug that time I thought I might find Shergar. If I said split ends and an oily T-zone you might guess who am referring to.

Then, we delved into the unpredictable field of beauty services, on Dan Dan's insistence. He's always been a bit more cuticles to my follicles. Dermabrasion to my dandruff, so to speak. He came in telling me of this rep fella he'd made a deal with to buy 3-for-2 epilation needles and a botox starter kit for beginners. I wasn't sure we were ready for the non-surgical nip and tuck palaver that seemed to be sweeping the nation's salons at the time. To this day, I'm still more of an alkaline perm kind of guy. Weft and weave, or take your leave. After a few months, I had to put my hands up and admit it was damn good for business. Blow drys up front in my domain, placenta injections in the back of the salon, courtesy of Dan Dan. We had it cooking, and frequently had to turn punters away, as a crowd attracts a crowd and all that.

I've always been lousy with money, whether I've had it or not. A man has his forte, but keeping a track of hard cash has never been mine. Dan Dan held all the cards...business, credit, all the other kinds, to boot. He started spending less time in the salon, all in the name of brokering deals, focusing on finance, and networking the industry. Those were the days when I thought sleeping partners in business was the same as shagging partners. I learnt otherwise later on page 42 of *Business for Dummies*. I was riding on a crest of a wave, but as they say, naïve is as naïve does.

Nothing was ever the same after the day the TV producers walked through the salon door with their notions of us being a setting for a reality show. They tell you they'll edit out the bad stuff, and slot in a satisfied client's smiling face and terrifically coiffured barnet every eight and a half minutes. They tell you a midweek daytime slot on a cable channel nobody's ever heard of will attract the right type of clientele. They tell you, above all, that they won't...make it into a freak show.

It became a cult classic, though not in the way folk fondly remember *Bewitched* or *The Wacky Races*. Think more Housewives of Bearsden mixed with Queer as *Real* Folk. I swear they were trying to edit me into some OTT scissor-wielding Alan Carr, my wild constitution a subplot to every episode. Dan Dan was sculpted into a Paul Hollywood-type silver god, with an unflappable temperament. They said they were trying to make it as 'real' as possible. But it turns out there is such a thing as bad publicity when a colonic irrigation gone wrong is caught on tape and edited to buggery.

The whole episode put pressure on us as a couple. They let the cameras roll during the catfighting and kicking of barber's chairs, and even asked us to tone it up, saying it was doing wonders for viewing figures. There were rumours an Israeli network channel wanted to buy the rights and broadcast it after dark. I'd visions of Dana International dubbing me in the voice-overs. Though let's be frank, I was all about making it big up the West End, not the Middle East.

Freaks camped outside the salon door overnight to be first in for a demi-wave they didn't need nor want. The fan mail was just sick, and I mean *pure* sick. The store cupboard became a holding room for the fruit cakes wanting their five minutes of fame but doing something ultimately obscene, and by the by, freaky. And when I say *holding room*, I mean it was the room we held them in until the fuzz came.

When celebrity life comes-a-knocking you tend to take your eye off the ball. Fame can do funny things to people, it's true. I protested to the hilt that I wanted none of it, but the night we were sat across from Colin and Justin at the Scottish Hairdresser Awards I knew I'd found my station in the murky limelight. Dan Dan was invited to more forays with Glasgow's luminaries and dignitaries than me, only due to what I decided was his handsome default. I'd stay back in the salon with the camera crew and producers, full heads of foils and bleached moustaches a go-go.

Something I always prided myself in was I never missed a day's work in my life. I once did a full bridal party with tennis elbow and a row of thumb blisters. But one morning I keeled over with an awful case of gastric lurgy right in the middle of an angular razor cut, on a filming day too. A Glasgow cleansing truck had got itself wedged between a Ford Transit and a Royal Mail van, meaning no ambulances could get down our one-way street as I lay prone on the salon floor. The producer, the cameraman and the sound mixer carted me down the street to their equips van, all jumping in with a quick *avanti* to the Royal Infirmary. I protested that I hated hospitals with a vengeance, ever since the stitches burst after my appendix op. I screamed the place down that the only way I'd go was if we picked up Dan Dan en route from our house. Bent over with sweats and cramps, I waited in the van as Patsy, the sound lassie, ran up the garden path. Just as she was about to give the front door a good bang, it swung open. I thought Dan Dan had sensed my pain in an ESP kinda way and was at the ready to hold my clammy hand. I rolled over on my makeshift ambulance bed, trying to keep my belly from vomiting for the fifth time when two silhouettes appeared in the doorway. There was no mistaking Dan Dan's towering frame, and as he took a step down the stoop he moved aside to reveal the skinny little rattlebones of no other than Johnny Nova. I would've boaked had the nausea not got there first. Patsy, with her boom mic still attached to her back, made a lunge before I rolled right off the trolley as if

God's hand and a dose of gravity had dropped on me.

I came back round in the infirmary, with my arse hanging out the back of one of those hospital gowns that never covers your cheeks if unblessed with a big butt and *can*not lie. I wasn't sure how long I'd been out for, but I realised quick-sharp it couldn't have been that long as the first vision I saw was Patsy, still wearing that red Berghaus fleece of hers. A good crimson rag to an enflamed bull she'd make any day. She stood at her usual three-foot distance and as I cranked my neck and looked to the ceiling there was the boom mic hovering over me like an auld fat squirrel at the end of a selfie stick.

Bloody cheek so it was, they kept the cameras still rolling...and do you know, it became our most-watched episode ever. But then again, Chrissy Scissorhawns on his deathbed is still a top attraction, know?

Ah, the Lonesome Blip

Ah've just this very moment come oot fae my AA meetin. Ah must admit it wis wan ae the better wans. Wee Jean, who claims twenty years of sobriety and still the need fur attendin a meetin oan a weekly basis, likes tae get talkin aboot "the sources of one's dependency" and "the foundations of one's addiction" and aw that malarky. She's a nice wee wummin is Jean, though sometimes she likes tae over-analyse the world and its dug a bit too much if ye ask me. But she's wan ae they psychologists, ey sportin a slick coiffure alang wae a big gypsy froack. Since aw that probin and dissectin is how she makes a crust, Ah tend tae let her aff. Anywiy, credit where credit's due cause the night she got the baw rollin alang recallin the first time we reckoned the booze wis gonnae play a big role in oor lives.

Fur me that wan wis easy, so Ah piped up...

15th ae June 1996 wis the day it aw turnt soor plooms fur yours truly. Ah'd only jist turnt seventeen, and Ah wouldnae have remembered the date so vividly if it hadnae been the day Scotland were playin England in the Euro Championships.

Boy oh boy, dae yees remember, there wis a build-up and a hauf tae that game. It wis wan ae they sportin occasions when it feels like five million people really get the gither as wan nation. Well, if we cannae dae it against the auld enemy at oor ain national sport, whit chance have *we* got?

Anywiy, Ah wisnae in too good a state back then. Well, tae be fair, Ah'm no any great shakes noo aw these years later, but that's another story. Fur noo, Ah'll try and stick tae the wan tale, cause wance Ah go aff oan a tangent there's no stoappin masel.

Ye see, back in the day Ah hadnae stuck in at school. And Ah'd been dabblin aboot wae Class Bs fur a while, which had accumulated in a whole set ae paranoias and delusions. Whit's merr, ye could say Ah wisnae the coolest kid tae hang aboot wae roon oor scheme neither. And the lassies...Jesus, maist ae them jist looked the other wiy across the street if they saw me comin. Wae ma Da workin doon south that week, there Ah wis, a lonesome blip in the sea ae they five million beatin hearts, a tattered soul with naebody Ah could call a real pal. Well, that's no entirely true, and afore Ah have yees greetin in yer ginger, aw this leads me oan tae where it aw kicked aff in my mind wae whit Jean had got us startit oan.

So the wiy it aw began careerin aff the rails wis like this... Aboot hauf an hour before the game wis due tae start that beltin Saturday efternoon, Ah'd nipped doon tae the Spar, and the contents of whit Ah came back wae in a poly bag wouldnae, well, take long tae be my new best muckers fae that day forward. Mind you, Ah hadnae planned it like that, right enough. Ah didnae buy those three cans ae Holsten Pils, four Dry Blackthorns and a cheeky boatle ae Thunderbird jist tae get blootered. Really, Ah didnae. Tae begin wae, Ah bought them cause Ah got a real buzz ae gettin served in the coarner shoap, and also cause that's whit folks dae, in't it, tae watch the fitba...get the cargo in.

Only Ah didnae see it at that point. Ah didnae see it comin how much Ah wid come tae depend oan those cans and boatles, and the hunners like them that were tae follow that day. Ah hadnae been a big boozer up tae that point. As Ah said tae ye previous, Ah wis merr intae the Class Bs. Ah can aw but remember those hazy days when Ah couldnae get oot my bed withoot knowin there wis a wee wrap waitin fur me oan the bedside table. Ah could go oan and oan aboot my dabblin in aw that, but this isnae my narcotics and amphetamines yarn.

Noo, wae ten minutes afore kick aff, Ah had wan ae my better brainwaves. Ah remembered Ah had a wee drap ae blackcurrant cordial in the fridge, leftover fae Christ knows when. Maist folk wid probably no touch a boatle that had its best before date rubbed aff wae a multitude ae hawns er a period ae time, but there wis me thinkin how hardcore Ah wis, makin a cocktail wae this cordial that had been oan the turn fur the better part ae two years. Ah grabbed my Clyde Wan mug tumbler my Auntie Senga had allegedly begged Tiger Tim fur wan time and proceeded tae fill hauf ae it wae a Holsten and the other hauf wae a Blackthorn.

Ah'd tried a few resultin Diesels wan night doon the club. Ah wis telt the week efter that Ah wis dancin aboot like a loon tae *Common People* by ra Pulp. Helluva surprise that wis, considerin Ah couldnae stomach that Jarvis Cocker wan at the time. Ah cannae remember a hing aboot that night tae this day, so Ah guess in my deep doon consciousness Ah knew gettin stuck intae the Diesel again was aw aboot gettin steamin oot my nut efter aw.

Ah took a few sips tae make wiy fur the cordial. And so wae the full mug in wan haun and a multi-pack ae salt and vinegar Discos under my other erm, Ah wis ready fur the kick aff.

Through tae my bedroom Ah wis jist in time tae get an earful ae John Motson, or whitever English twat wis commentatin that day, gie oot his so-called unbiased tripe followed by the line ups...*McKimmie, McKinlay, Spencer.* Aye, the kind ae players tae drive the fear ae God up any Englishman. Alangside my desire tae see us hump those Sassenach bastards, my yearnin tae see whit kind ae buzz the liquid content in my grasp wis gonnae gie me coincided nae end.

Ah remember thinkin at the time how proud Ah wis no tae be an alkie like my Da and the family ae wee jakeys up my close. Hauf wiy tae bein a junkie, mibbaes. But up tae that point the booze hadnae got a haunle oan me. Though thinkin aboot it noo, hauf a tumbler ae that magic diesel yon day and Ah was jumpin oan the slippery slide tae boozy heaven— no forgettin the boozy hell that wis tae come wae it—wae two big size nines.

Aye, hauf a tumbler doon, and there Ah wis comin awiy wae my ain version ae *Football's Coming Home* alang the lines ae *Yer goin out, yer goin out, Gazza's fuckin shite!* or some blabberin rabble like that. Ah cursed that Frank Skinner tae a hellish demise, and threw a few obscenities at the sight ae his wee hairy sidekick…ye know, the other wan naebody can remember the name ae. Ah grabbed my lion rampant aff the waw and wrapped it roon masel in a code ae pride. When *Flower ae Scotland* came oan fur the anthems, Ah stood oan the bed and belted it oot my windae. When *God Save The Queen* startit up, Ah went fur a slash and pretended Ah wis pishin oan her heid.

And then the game kicked aff and Ah got toarn intae my first packet ae Discos. Til this day, Ah love the wiy they crisps just coat yer mooth in a film ae vinegary salt. Never mind a jammy doughnut or a fruity pastille, try eatin them bad boys withoot lickin yer lips. Feelin fully nourished efter two packets, and reachin the dregs ae the first ae my Diesels wae the scoreline still at nil-nil, ye could say Ah wis quite satisfied wae my lot.

It wis then Ah realised somethin that Ah refused tae admit at the time, but Ah'am big enough tae admit noo—the fact Ah wisnae in it fur jist the wan pint mug ae happy juice. By that point Ah already wanted merr. Ah knew Ah wis in the midst ae losin another wee pocket ae brain cells, but Ah wis happy tae trade them fur the sensation ae no feelin trapped within the four waws ae my room fur wance. Wae the Class Bs, Ah just went radio rental, makin up imaginary pals tae talk tae, alang wae dealin wae aw the mad zombie wans Ah thought were comin tae get me fae behind the waws. At least wae the drink Ah wis beginnin tae understaun that maist ae yer heid is still yer heid, no the wiy Ah wis used tae losin it afore in wan big chemical smog.

Aye, somehow wan part Holsten, wan part Blackthorn and that wee smidge ae ootdated cordial made me forget my dire existence and pushed awiy the image that every other soul in the country wis sittin wae hunners ae pals in a pub, or gathered roon a B&Q barbeque laughin their heids aff that sunny summer's efternoon. Efter aw, Ah remember thinkin tae masel, Ah'd found my ain wee companions, wans wae merr fluidity than Castrol GTX, and wae merr buzz than huvin a wasp in yer lug.

When the ref blew the whistle fur hauf time wae the score still at nil-nil, Ah decided tae pop open the Thunderbird, which acted as a lovely sweet tonic between the soorness ae the Diesels. It should've belang in the fridge for the forty-five minutes previous, but the fact the boatle had sat oan the bedside table fur that long gied it a sickly room temperature that had me stickin my tongue oot fur relief.

Luckily, another packet ae Discos sorted that oot. Efter a few big gulps ae my Thunderbird, Ah pit the boatle in the fridge fur later oan. Even at that early stage, in whit's been a long process, Ah wisnae fur wastin wan drap.

Oan my wiy back fae the kitchenette, Ah grabbed a packet ae KP Dry Roasteds jist as a wee chiynge fae the Discos. Back in my bedroom, Ah proceeded tae fill my tumbler, and my boots, wae another hyper-

15

speed brew. The cameraman panned roon the slopes ae Wembley and zoomed in oan a bunch ae ugly coupins wae they stupit white plastic bowler hats and faces ye'd jist want tae slap if ever ye had the displeasure ae meetin them in the street. And then Ah caught a wee glimpse ae the mighty Tartan Army foot soldiers. Better lookin fur wan thing, and showin chin-chimney Jimmy Hill, and aw his cronies jist how tae party fur another.

Another great thing Ah wis noticin for the first time wis the merr ye drink, the merr ye think. And at that point Ah really did think Scotland wis gonnae dae it. Up goes the optimism levels nae end. Noo, the second hauf ae the match proceeded tae be a different kettle ae fish. The first hauf Ah'd jist been gettin settled. For wan thing, gettin bolshie wae a TV screen in a room wae naebody else in it is fuckin inane when ye stoap tae think aboot it. Even some tosser arguin back is got tae be better than yer ain solitary jabber rattlin aff the waws. Ah downed my tumbler a bit faster tae help forget aboot aw that...

And then oot ae the blue, Ah looked up tae see an English baw comin in fae the right wing, and the next thing Ah knew that fanny, Shearers heid wis oan the end ae it tae pit it in the back ae the net. Like my four million, nine hunner and ninety-nine thoosand, nine hunner and ninety-nine compatriots, Ah couldnae believe it.

Ah wis determined no tae let that wee insignificance get me doon in the dumps. Efter aw, Ah'd talked masel intae thinkin, it's the Scottish wiy, in't it?

Triumph er adversity? Hope er reality merr like. Jist a wee, tiny glitch in the proceedins, Ah tried tae convince masel. Ah mind it wis roon aboot this point Ah went through a wee phase ae the flushes. Ah mean it wis a warm day an aw that, but whit Ah needed wis a goal tae help let oot aw that pent-up frustration and liquor-fuelled headiness. Like Ah says, Ah wisnae a big boozer, so the title ae *Two Can Dan* wis aboot the measure ae it.

Ah bopped up and doon oan my bed fur aw ae thirty seconds til Ah wis practically cream-crackered. Efter that Ah mind prancin roon the room a bit tae shake the anxiousness. Nane ae it helped, so Ah sat doon fur a few minutes efter that, tryin tae sit cross-legged. Ah wis decidedly locked in a thick malaise. Ah felt bloody marvellous but helluva restless at wan and the same time. Ah championed that sensation in my heid by poppin open the Dry Roasteds. Free fallin nuts that somehow missed my gapin mooth landed oan the duvet, oan the rug, and wan even drapped intae wan ae the Holsten empties. It wis a sign, Ah wis sure ae it. If Ah gubbins like me could get a peanut intae a fuckin beer can withoot tryin, then Scotland could score a goal when they're giein it a hunner and twinty per cent.

As Ah grew with that belief in mind, Ah got doon oan my knees and pit my heid right up tae the TV screen wae my haunches restin oan my heels tae focus aw the will Ah possessed oan Scotland gettin the equaliser. But d'ye know whit? Ah widnae recommend that cause tryin tae follow twinty-two wee pair ae legs runnin roon a bit ae lush lawn in such close proximity as that jist makes yer heid swim. The wee figurines ae John Collins and Andy Goram Ah'd got oot the cereal packets, and sat oan my makeshift telly shelf, looked as nervous as a couple ae judges caught wae their pants doon.

Ah then sat back a bit, grabbed my mug and made up another cocktail, as Ah didnae want tae be empty-haunded when the moment that had tae come, actually came. Ah had a right good swig oot ae that wan, decidin that even the taste wis mind-blowin if ye gulp enough moothfuls ae it in rapid succession.

As Ah looked back up at the screen, aw Ah saw wis Juke Box Durie go tae grun wae the aid ae that big eejit, Tony Adams' flailing leg. *Ya Beauty!* The ref pointed tae the penalty spot right away and Ah jumped up like a fuckin loon. Ah wis as proud ae masel fur avoidin unnecessary spillage as much as Ah wis ae Scotland fur giein us aw hope ae an equaliser.

Ah jist didnae know whit tae do wae masel awthegither in that wee moment. Ah didnae have a sofa in my bedroom tae hide behind. Ah didnae have another soul tae grab oantae. And Ah didnae have any nails tae bite neither. Ah took wan last big gulp tae drain my mug, and decided in aw my wisdom tae get as close as Ah could tae the action by grabbin oantae the telly shelf at either side. The shelf wis really no a shelf at aw mind. It wis actually a door aff an oven, held up wae black shoelaces nailed intae the waw wae a couple ae they brass bracket numbers.

So anywiy, back doon oan my knees Ah had my hawns gripped roon my piece ae makeshift furniture as Gary McAllister picked up the baw and placed it oan the penalty spot. Ah could practically feel the nation gasp as wan as the camera focused oan Macca, a hero in the makin, haudin five million heartbeats in his left fit.

Suddenly Ah started tae feel pins and needles in my ain feet, followed by a right attack ae the sweats. Ah could see my knuckles goin white right in front ae me, as a fervent hot flush rose fae my chist, up tae my cheeks and reached a fiery climax in my foreheid. The room started tae spin like Ah wis oan the waltzers, and fur a split second Ah swear Ah wis seein stars oan the wallpaper. Jist as Ah wis tellin masel tae get it the gither and be thankful it wisnae zombies fae oot the waw, Ah could see Macca make his runny up tae the penalty spot. The next thing Ah knew in my moment ae anticipation, hope and anxiety wis the shelf startin tae come awiy fae the waw wae such a force ae weight Ah couldnae react quick enough tae save masel. The last thing Ah remember wis thinkin that Ah really wis seein things as Ah wis sure Ah saw the baw move aff the penalty spot jist as Macca wis aboot tae kick...

It wis dark when Ah came roon. At first, Ah didnae have a clue where the hell Ah wis. But Ah realised wan thing quick sharpish—that my whole boady wis in pure bits as Ah lay oan the carpet wae a 28 inch Grundig oan tap ae my chist. My size nines still felt numb as if the circulation had been cut aff fae them. In a wiy Ah should've been bloody grateful cause if the telly had landed a fit lower Ah might have lost wan or even baith ae my baws, or at the very least no been able tae have weans efter that. Ah could feel my shins were bruised black and blue, presumably fae where the oven door had landed oan them. My fingers were aw skint at the knuckles as if Ah'd tried tae box the TV fae fallin oan tap ae me. My eyebaws were the only capable movin part ae me, wae my neck aw cranked in pain as Ah tried tae wriggle oot fae under my electrical adversary. Ah jist aboot managed tae turn my heid ninety degrees tae the left, although it wis killin me tae dae so. And there lyin oan my rug wis Andy Goram, his heid decapitated fae his boady. Next tae him lay a tangled shoelace wae a mangled bracket at the end of it, and a Holsten empty, its midriff crushed in the kerfuffle.

"JESUS JOHNNY!" Ah cried oot in pain, which unavoidably turnt intae laughter as Ah caught a glimpse ae masel in the mirror and the state ae my situation. Wance the laughter had died doon tae a cackle, my thoughts immediately turnt tae the penalty. Ah had been knocked oot by my ain fuckin telly the split second afore Macca had whacked it, in? Over the bar? Saved? Ah didnae know. Ah gave oot another scream. Wance ma echoes had faded intae the waws, Ah could hear a crackly wee voice fae oot in the hall. Ah couldnae work it oot at first, but Ah knew it wisnae my Da's dulcets and then Ah minded that Ah had the radio oan in the kitchenette earlier. Ah kept quiet as a moose, and strained my ear tae try and hear whit the DJ wis wafflin oan aboot. Whit? Whit wis that? Ah swore he said somethin aboot Gazza no bein able tae come back tae Glesga and somethin an aw aboot Uri Geller takin the plaudits. Whit the fuck wis aw that aboot, Ah wondered,. lyin there in my state ae distress and sufferance. Ah couldnae decide if my ears were hallucinatin tae at that point, but Ah had a wee inklin that aw hadnae gone tae plan fur oor players and foot soldiers alike. It wis too quiet oot in the close, and oot in the streets tae. Dejected and wrigglin in pain, Ah cranked my heid tae the right, and whit Ah saw deid ahead in front ae me wis a wee collection ae dynamite that's incidentally led me tae be staunin here ootside the AA hall, sharin wae yees this yarn. Aye, right there in front ae me wis the poly bag wae a Holsten and a Blackthorn pokin oot. The boatle ae cordial wis lyin jist oan tap ae the bed, and fortunately jist in erm's reach. *Ya dancer!* Ah mind laughin tae masel. Aw these years later Ah wisnae sure if it wis a small or massive mercy, but at the time it wis the only sight that wis gonnae cheer me up considerin the circumstances.

It wisnae until a couple ae days later when Ah managed tae get my poor, battered boady oot the door intae civilisation that Ah realised whit happened that sunny, Saturday efternoon at Wember-fucker-ley.

And like aw alcoholics dae, Ah'm blamin the sources of wan's dependency and the foundations of wan's addiction oan somethin other than my ain responsibility. So fur the record, Ah'm blamin it purely oan the heid ae that spoon-bendin wee muppet, Uri Geller. If it hadnae been fur him Ah widnae have headed straight fur the Spar that same mornin.

Wee Jean wisnae fur huvin any of it, but ye should've seen her face when Ah also telt her whit Ah'd went through tryin tae reach my Clyde Wan tumbler.

Oh Mo

Oh Mo, I could've died when Granny
slung that terry-towelling
valance over her shoulder
and cawed you the wee half-caste boy

Eyes down Ma went,
You cannae go about saying that
in public these days, wiping her
imaginary oose fae the mantel

Alexa, Granny shouts
all two and a bit feet away,
What are you supposed to say insteed
of half-caste noo-adays?

Alexa doesn't have a scooby,
flashing her blue crown
no delay, she tells the room
I am having trouble understanding you

If you need to ask whit's-her-face
tae keep ye right Granda pipes up
over the *Racing Post*
the world's gone stark raving,
nae danger

D'ye know Mo, if Granny had you down
as sallow that would be you exotic,
somebody tae be envious over
cause sallow means ye take
a right good tan in summer

Muhammad Ali, Granda says
his two-penneth no quite finished
Flew like a butterfly, stung like a bee him
Aye but Da, her wee Muhammed
is no *that* coloured, so he's no

Am just about apoplectic now, Mo

Even dreamt last night
Granny and Granda were invited
onto *Long Lost Family,*
but the person who found them
wanted to gie them both back

It's their generation, Ma goes
with that nae-words-needed look of hers
She once told me of Granny's
wee mental rolodex
for what fits her idea of dark,
but handsome (whitever a rolodex is)

She says Sidney Poitier can dae
no wrang, neither can Harry Belafonte—
Granda swoons at the mention of
Shirley Bassey and swears
Sammy Davis Jr was pun for pun
more talented than Sinatra

Granny says she cannae mind
whit wee Muhammad you are
and it must be like ma's and da's
all cawing their weans Jimmy,
loads of them all over the place
with the same name

Beam me up, Alexa

Or whit aboot Sammys? Granda says
There wis five Sammys on our street
at one time,
Two up the same close, says Granny
Aye, was one no a set of twins?

Do you ever listen to yourselves,
I say just loud enough for Granda
to hear and Granny to wonder
what just went over her head—
Whit's bugged her mince, well?

Caw them the fossil twins don't you, Mo?
What's the difference between
Neanderthal and Jurassic?
We laughed at that for ages, didn't we?
About 65 dillion years, give or take

Ma will get the chap at the door,
she's no reason to leave you
standing out in the dreich
So in you'll come, all tucked in at the seams
and pure impenetrable

Well if it's no your…*wee Sammy*
Granny'll say, with a wink as brazen
as I've seen on her all week
Granda'll look up, maybe hoping
to see the Rat Pack dauner in
and do a turn in the front room

Alexa's playing up again
—Amazon's glitch in the matrix
Sorry I'm really having trouble
understanding you right now

Aye, no kiddin

Beam us up Mo, you and me,
gonnae beam us all the way up!

2020 Minus Thirty

We shoe-gazed our way through happy Mondays
that year the Clyde's heart ran culture
through its awarded veins.
Tie-dyed waist up, acid-washed hips down
we danced on inspiral carpets
as Mandela flew the coop to freedom.

Seattle spawned a generation x,
just fit enough to be dragged screaming
and shouting into the mosh pit—
where we stood on a precipice,
angst-ridden, apathetic
yet full of the century's last flurry of sonic youth.

Nessun Dorma kept us awake all summer,
none shall sleep as Desert Shield rose,
curtains fell, a chip off the old Berliner's block.
With a link in the chunnel, a kink in the ozone,
Weegies sat back, smiles better
licking our ice – ice – babies.

Hubble let Orion Nebula shine like a star,
while toil and poll tax trouble
burst Maggie's veritable bubble.
Gazza gret a river, Imelda racketed up shoes
—by the score, they buzzed like she had
whizz strapped to her toes.

They came to our dear green place for the cultuur,
strike a pose Glesga, there's nothing to it.
Home alone with yon goodfellas and real gone kids,
pride was found and grammar lost,
Auld Reekie, U Can't Touch this,
glas cau, be it true, Nothing Compares 2 U.

A Future Not What It Used To Be

Along you came, impeccably dressed
in your second-hand vest,
my muse, my jezebel
and my mecca—
my driving seat on the double decka

A roulette thumping,
free spin humping,
three-cherry jackpot fantasia

Accumulators, by a nose,
correct score, double or fold
any each way—but lose,
you and me in our daily hustle

Drag me out at two in the morning
you would and hours, days,
months in your presence
became my pain and my remedy
dirty deeds done, like a shotgun
needs an outcome

Like a vice grip to my brain
my heart dripped impure,
scruples flew through windows
and isolation settled, til one day
you took the shirt off my back

and left me feeling more burnt out
than a row of Suzuki Swifts
on a Possil Park side street
—my face tripping me enough
to turn a Baileys Viennetta sour

But I see you now,
at least in my rearview mirror,
I see you now

Like a sly shiver waiting for a spine to run up
my spine
my morals
my bank account

Hit my rock bottom,
but bounced off the tarmac,
decided you don't give
bang-bang for my buck no more

From this day forward
my past wheels of misfortune
no longer define,
as without you in it,
my future is not what it used to be

Aye, this is my Dear John letter,
from me to you—
I've signed it and you'll find it
on the change machine
of an old penny arcade

Daddy Uncool

See at home, I've got this goldfish bowl, almost full to its brim it is with pesos, lire, riyals and those bigger coins from Africa. Sits on my bookshelf it does, and guess what...it's only going to be topped up with the return of Daddy today, so it is. Waiting at the big Glasgow airport, like we do every time he's finished a dig, Mum, Lucy and I watch the planes come and go, our cheeks pressed against the big windows.

"Does Daddy really walk through a gate, Mummy?" Lucy asks, tapping Mum's arm with her wrist. "Like a gate on a farm?" As she stares down the long corridor, where Daddy appears from behind the big frosty screens, I stare at her, my face showing I reckon what she's asked is the silliest question ever. She pretends not to see me.

When I was Lucy's age, I kept my coins in a jam jar Mum had washed all the stickiness out of. My faves are the American quarters, and the ones with the holes taken from the middle. I used to pretend my dimes and nickels had once been in the palms and pockets of famous actors and singers. That's where all the famous people live, so I reckon there's a good chance they've used my coins to buy a cup of coffee, or make a phone call, just like they do in the movies.

Daddy is an archeologist, so he has no time for celebs, but he says he'll bring me back a holey dollar one day, because that's *the holy grail.*

It wasn't long before I had to swap the jam jar for an old chipped vase. I didn't like the scummy bits that stuck to the inside of its base, and I always made sure my favourites never sank to the bottom and became blemished by whatever Mum's daffodils had left behind.

It's the start of summer, and at the end of it, I'll be going to the big school. If I hear my aunties or neighbours or anybody talk about *wee fish and big ponds* and *big fish and wee ponds* one more time I think I'll scream. They all say such stupid stuff as if they know what it's like. I suppose they do. But I'm surprised they're not all too old to remember.

Luckily, Mum doesn't say any stupid stuff like that, even when she is being her silly self. I much prefer the make-believe and guessing games she encourages me and Lucy to play. Why do they always seem more funny at the airport?

I like it best when we come on a Sunday. The airport is just as busy on Sundays as any other day, but more people walk around in T-shirts and flip-flops, even in winter. Even Lucy sees how silly flip-flops look in December. On weekdays there are too many tired-looking men with serious faces carrying briefcases. They make me feel sad, sometimes even annoyed, because airports should be happy places for only happy people. I like the daddies who let their children jump on the luggage trolleys and wheel them around like they're allowed to just because they're special and going on summer holiday. I like that, when adults act silly, but it doesn't look uncool at the same time.

"I think the man over there," Mum says, "in the Hawaiian shirt runs a bank." Somehow I know what a Hawaiian shirt is, but Lucy has that guessing face on her. "Though today," Mum adds, "he's downed tools for two weeks and off to the sun."

"What tools do people in banks use, Mummy?" Lucy asks.

"Spades and shovels, to bury all your money," I say, tickling my sister in the ribs.

"People who do the most boring thing for fifty weeks of the year go a bit crazy when it comes to their two weeks off," Mum says, smiling. I love how Mum teaches us lots of things, like in just one state-ment. Like I didn't know before how many weeks there were in a whole year, and I certainly didn't know that's what men who run banks look like when they go on holiday. I feel happy for the bank manager, but maybe a bit jealous too, though only because he's likely to have a bigger coin collection than me.

Daddy's been away for over six months this time, in Turkey. He's a very important man, so he is. Some-times he slips into the language of the places he's been to, but it always just sounds like gibberish to me. We've come to the airport early and like to spend the day here, like the amount of time you might spend at the fun fair or Ayr beach. Mum never makes us a big lunch or lets us eat too many sweets, as she likes me and Lucy to have big appetites for when Daddy arrives and we go to the airport restaurant and he asks the waitress for "big steaks all round."

Mum picks up her puzzle magazine and starts a crossword. Lucy always carries her pens for whatever occasion a pen might be needed. She snuggles in tight to Mum's side and pretends to help with the clues. She's such a sook sometimes, and the only time she isn't hanging off Mum is when Daddy is home. Then, Daddy is hanging off Mum, and Lucy is hanging off Daddy. I hang off no one because I'm not a sookie Sue. Two boys in the seats behind us are having a competition about which of their mums is the most dumb.

"Your maw is soooo stupid," one of them says, "she can't work out the pricing system in Poundland."

"Well no, your momma is so dumb, when she went for a blood test…she failed."

I sit silent, listening for a while to their kiddie-on insults. Boys are a pain most of the time, but somehow they're funnier than girls. It's the one-liners I suppose. I'm never telling them I think that though. Boys' heads are big enough for this world.

When Lucy gets bored, we count all the different airline logos out on the runways. I get the feeling I'd be pretty good if I was tested on them, like in school. I'm proud to know a British Airways logo from a Lufthansa, even at a far-off distance. I know this because of Daddy, even though he never taught me it one-to-one.

It's nearly time. Nearly. The planes Daddy arrives on are hardly ever on time, and never ever early. The arrival time says 4:45pm on the big board, but we know we won't see him for another half hour at least. But that's okay. It makes it more exciting, our waiting for Daddy's face to appear among the strangers.

Mum packs up all her magazines as Lucy hangs off her like washing on a windy day, and I race toward the start of the corridor. He doesn't have his own walk, Daddy doesn't. Not like Uncle Harvey or Mr Davis, my old school janitor. They have walks you'd spot a mile away. Though I suppose Daddy is just normal because he doesn't have a gammy leg, or a nervous dispensation, or whatever grown-ups call it.

Mum and Lucy catch up and we stand in the middle of the entrance, not caring that we're taking up lots of space, or that all the people have to walk round us. They are just a wave of weird faces...I suppose like curtains, they can just separate and open up the figure of Daddy to me. More of them come and pass by. A boy rubbing his eyes, holding a teddy bear. A woman with a big floral dress, who'd nicely fit aside the bank manager. A man with a deep tan, a gold watch and a briefcase. A man that's like Da...looks like Dad...*it is* Daddy. But it isn't. What's different? It's not his walk...

"Daddy, what have you done with your moustachy?" Lucy asks, leaping in front of me, just missing my toes.

Daddy scoops Lucy up with one arm like she's a feather doll. "I lost it in the desert, sweetheart," he says, reaching forward to give Mum a peck right on the lips. "Don't it make your old man look more handsome?"

35

"Yes dear, quite the surprise," Mum answers, "reminds me of our winching days."

Daddy looks down at me. I know he knows that I know he knows I'm way too old to be lifted into his other arm like he used to. Me in one arm, Lucy in the other, Mum pushing the trolley, keeping up behind us. I realise I haven't welcomed him, or given him the smile I save only for airport days. I've never seen Daddy without his moustache before. He looks...not the same. Not older, not younger, just kinda ...well, different. And trust Lucy to notice and say something first. You couldn't shackle her mouth with a muzzle if you tried.

"Well Kiddo, doesn't Daddy get a big smacker, eh?" Daddy lets Lucy slide down his side like a monkey down a drainpipe. Her skirt rises up and her knickers show. He bends over a long way to pull her skirt back to its right length, all the time looking at me for my answer.

"Briony! What's wrong with you?" Lucy shouts. "It's Daddy...Daddy's home!"

"Shush, shush. There, there, Poppet," Daddy says, stroking Lucy's fringe away from her eyes.

"Hello Daddy," I say, almost in whisper. I'm waiting for Lucy to say something really loud, making my words sound even quieter.

It's Mum who speaks. "Righto, let's get out the way of the hordes." Her words are there beside me, but I'm not really hearing them as I stand rooted to the spot staring at Daddy...Daddy the Strange.

"Daddy's lost his tashy, Daddy's lost his tashy,"

Lucy sings. There's no tune to her voice as she grabs his arm, pulling him away from the corridor.

Sitting at the table in the restaurant which gives the best view of the runways, I watch as Daddy orders the usual "one well done, two medium rare and one rare enough to look like it's still moving on the plate," from the waitress.

"And a big banana split too, Daddy," Lucy demands, as the waitress gathers up the menus we didn't even open.

"Only if you eat all your dinner, Poppet," Mum says, right on cue.

"Hm-mm," Daddy nods with wide eyes.

The whole time he does this, I'm staring—staring at his face. Without his moustache, I notice the big space between his nose and lips. It's all sweaty, but the rest of his face seems too dry. From the angle I'm sitting he can't see me looking at him, or pretends he can't. I pinch my nose and feel how small and round, and close it is to my lip. Daddy's nose is big with long gapes for nostrils. Yip, without a moustache, it seems Daddy has the biggest nose I've ever seen. It's bony and kind of crooked, but not like a boxer's though. It looks foreign to me. It feels weird that I recognise some of Daddy, but not all of him.

Lucy slams herself against the high back of her chair as if she's in a huff, then wriggles her bum until she's up straight again. I don't know anyone who can cause such a big commotion around themselves, even in silence.

"How's the holidays, Kiddo?" Daddy asks.

37

"Fine," I answer. If it was still term time I know Daddy would've asked, "how's school, Kiddo?" It's all the same.

Mum asks about Daddy's flight and the duty free and the rate between the pound and the dollar. Daddy gets paid in American dollars. I understand how exchange rates work because of that. All the time he's talking with Mum, he keeps making little glances at me, as if figuring out whether I'm being odd with him. I don't like to play games with Daddy usually, but somehow I feel like I'm getting him back for looking different to me by being quiet, and keeping him guessing.

"Look at all my pens, Daddy..." Lucy shouts, laying her gel pens on the table. "Help me make a rainbow, like you did before."

I realise Lucy isn't mad at Daddy, not like I am, for changing...Red. I suppose, after all, she's too young and whatever Daddy does, to her, the sun will always shine out of his bum...Orange. I feel like a bit of a scaredy-cat for not speaking up, and for being all strange with him, and even Mum looks at me as though I've done something bad...Yellow. It's just like Lucy to take over and get all Daddy's attention with her sweetness...Green. Okay, so, if I just sit here and look sad with Daddy and the whole world, I'm not going to feel better...Blue. I guess I could forgive him, maybe. I mean, it's not as though he's ran off with another family, is it? Not like Chantelle Bailey's dad across the road...Indigo. Yip, I understand. I really do. When Daddy comes home for his break, good things happen for us. Days out and new toys, and Mum is happier too. We're lucky for that...Purple.

"There," I say to Lucy, handing over the last pen, "now you've got a lovely rainbow."

Mum and Daddy look at me as if I'm the best big sister in the world. I can't wait for dinner now.

After the banana splits, we head off to the concourse for the taxi home. Mum can't drive, so our car stays in the lock-up when Daddy's away. It's amazing how Daddy knows every taxi driver in the world. What's even more amazing is that they're all called *Jim*. Daddy and all those Jims just seem to get on like a big house on fire.

I really have decided to forgive Daddy for shaving off his moustache. I might even get used to it. I wonder what Mum could do to make herself look really different. I suppose it's easier for men in that way because they have so many add-ons to play about with.

It's still light outside as we arrive home and getting out the taxi, I see Chantelle playing on her front step with the Labrador puppy I know has been bought to stop her temper tantrums in the middle of our street. I pretend not to look all proud when she stares, and I know, as if by magic, that all she sees is Daddy, and how, if she drew a picture of us, it would be of the perfect family inside a frame.

In the living room, I'm even more excited now than I was at the airport. Daddy's recent dig was his longest yet, which means I'll have new coins and wee trinkets I've never seen before to add to my collection.

Daddy plops into his armchair like a lead weight being thrown onto a bean bag. I sit watching as he undoes the buttons on his shirt cuffs and rolls them up his tanned arms. "Ah, home-sweet-home," he says, breathing out each word slowly.

"The usual, Faither?" Mum asks in her kiddie-on voice as she pulls me away from Daddy to give him some space. We all know the *usual* means an Irish Coffee and a fat cigar.

"T'would indeed be delightful, dear," Daddy sighs. He sounds like a character from the Charles Dickens book I've just read...so uncool, but I'll let him off.

Lucy comes running in from the downstairs bathroom with her skirt stuck into her knickers.

"You wash your hands?" I ask her.

She looks at her palms, frowns, and runs back out.

I laugh, because I know she's annoyed at the thought of missing out on anything that's going on in the living room.

"Guess what, Daddy," I say, as Daddy pretends he hasn't just closed his eyes for longer than two whole seconds.

"What, Daddy?" he says, rubbing his forehead.

"No serious. Guess what."

"What, Kiddo?"

"I've so many coins from all your digs away that I need a glass as big as a fishbowl now." It's my way of getting him to show what new coins he has for me.

"Still into the coin collecting, hmm?"

"Course," I say. "I'd never give them away, or spend

them even if they were worth a million pounds."

"Good on ya, Kiddo," he says yawning, his fingers linked and resting against his chest.

Just as Lucy returns, wiping her wet hands along the curtains and sofa, Mum comes through from the kitchen with the Irish Coffee and Daddy's special box of cigars. She has the look on her that says what a waste of time that was, as Daddy lets out one of his quiet little snores she knows won't be quiet or little in a few minutes.

The doorbell goes, and we all turn to see if it has woken Daddy at all. He lets out a wheezy snort, but nothing more. I pull myself away from the armchair towards the hallway. Through the glass, I can see the silhouette of Chantelle holding her puppy. I knew she couldn't stay away for too long...but really, only ten minutes we'd been in the door. Yip, ten whole minutes, she'd given herself. What's more, I reckon she tried counting the seconds on her doorstep *...one Mississippi, two Mississippi...* But Chantelle is the most easily distracted person I know, so I wouldn't bet a rupee she even made it to *four Mississ...*

I hover about the hallway for a second, letting her know I know she's waiting and bouncing on my doorstep. Lucy comes firing out of the living room, and on realising who's there, turns and marches back with a roll of the eyes. Lucy can't stand Chantelle and makes no secret of it when she insists Chantelle is "cruel and smelly," and that all the animals in her house have rabies. "What, even the fish?" Daddy once asked. "Hm-mm, even her piranhas have rabies!"

41

I open the door with all the laziness of a...well, really lazy thing.

"Say hello to Huxley, Miss Briony..." Chantelle says, wagging a tiny yellow paw eagerly. "Mr Huxley, say hello to Briony."

"Aren't puppies not meant to be out and about so young?" I ask. I don't know the ins and outs of how and when you're supposed to go about introducing puppies or kittens, any animal for that fact, to the world.

"Oh, that's right," Chantelle grins that grin of hers, "you wouldn't know about any of that, huh?" She's not daft, Chantelle, and as quick as lightning to remind me I'm not allowed a pet.

I peel my eyes enviously away from the gorgeously cute mound of fur in her arms. "Well, at least I'll never be bitten by one, or have my leg humped to death."

"Just shows what she knows, eh Mr Hux Huxley?" she says, rocking the puppy from side to side, giving it little Eskimo kisses.

This was going just how I imagined she'd planned it. I need something to get back at her...

Yeah, that was it...

Suddenly, I know what to do. "How about seeing something you've def-in-ite-ly never ever seen before?" The bait was laid, and I've known Chantelle since I was four, even though she goes to the other school. What I mean is, I know just how she's going to react. "Something you've never seen before, because even I ain't seen it before."

"What could you have to show me that's going to

42

top the arrival of Mr Huxley here, hmm?"

Perfect, and very much a Chantelle Bailey-like reaction, bouncing my question with another question. Will we always do this, even when we're old and thirty-something, I wonder? It's like Dare and Double Dare, and I like it. Bluff and Triple Bluff. Me and Chantelle are like, the experts.

"Just wait there and don't move," I say, knowing I've got to be firm to hold her attention.

"Oh okay," she says, with it a sigh that's so over the top it must've worked its way up from her toes.

I leave her waiting right there and tiptoe back into the living room. Mum has the volume up a bit louder than usual on the TV, though God knows why she wants to hear the newsreader's voice at that volume. How boring. If Daddy was awake he'd tell Mum not to rot her brain with mainstream news. And I'd get it (Lucy wouldn't) because I'm older...and so much wiser. Thank God for her colouring pens, they keep her occupied for hours, belly to the floor with her drawing books, as is now, right by Daddy's feet.

I creep behind the armchair and hope Chantelle's patience will hold out before she starts chapping on the door. Crouched down and out of sight I snatch Daddy's briefcase and wriggle backwards on my knees out the door. The briefcase is heavier than usual, giving my knees the grief of carpet burns. Once out in the hallway again, I open the front door and grab Chantelle's arm before she knows what's hit her.

"WHOA! Watch Mr Huxley's ears will you!"

"Shoosh and follow me, if you know what's good for you."

"Briony Marshall! Devil knows what the flip you're up to…"

I shoo Chantelle in front of me indicating the need to keep both her and Mr Huxley's heads low as we race past the living room window. Of course, old Mrs Carmichael just happens to be getting out of her old Mini the very same moment and eyes us suspiciously.

"Ignore her," I say, urging Chantelle into the close, "she'd have the police round if you were having a game of conkers in the street."

Out the close and round past the shed, we duck into my little cubby hole at the end of our garden. I pull the branches lower to keep unwanted eyes away. Sitting down, I place Daddy's briefcase on my knees, and Chantelle does the same with Mr Huxley.

"This better be good, Briony. And I hope that briefcase isn't where your dad keeps all his dirty pants."

"Will ye shoosh for all of two seconds...and keep the dog's paws away from the leather."

"Pete's sake!"

Daddy doesn't know I know the combination code, though it's true he's never kept it secret. I reckon he forgets how I'm old enough to be as smart as an adult. Smarter, HA!

"Three-One-Three, Open Sesame."

"Not exactly rocket science, is it?" Chantelle moans. Mr Huxley barks a little squeal, as if in agreement.

Plane tickets and luggage tags and Visa card receipts all scrunched up... jeez, Daddy sure isn't the tidiest. Sifting through contracts and papers, my heart starts beating fast. I know I'm only fingertips away from my treasure and wiping that smirk off Chantelle's face.

"You're gonna get yourself into trouble one of these days, Briony Marshall."

I'm just about to swipe at Chantelle for calling me by full name in that tone of voice again when my hand smooths over the first coin. I pull it out from under all the paper stuff and hold it up like it's a gold sovereign recovered from the depths of the earth. "That," I say, holding the coin up to Chantelle's nose, "is what you call a 'kuruş'. Lovely, isn't it?"

"How much is it worth, then?" Chantelle asks. I'm not surprised at this. Someone whose house doesn't always have bed sheets on the mattresses probably would think like that.

"That's not important," I say, twisting the coin toward the last beam of sunlight. "Do you have any idea where Turkey is, at all? Or what age this coin is, hmm?"

"Well can I hold it a minute?"

"Only if you don't let him lick it."

"Don't reckon Mr Huxley goes in for rusty old coins somehow."

"Hm-mm, whatever."

I know there's more to be found, I can hear the jingle from the bottom of the case. I spread my hand across the soft material inside and scoop up more

45

coins of different sizes and a few notes too. Before I have time to pull my hand out, the case lid falls onto my elbow. Pulling my arm free with a stash of treasure in hand, Chantelle's face lights up as if it were the mother of all her Christmases.

"All that must be like...over a hundred pounds or something." The gape in her mouth could catch flies.

"How many times do I have to tell you? It's not the value that's important...it's, well it's the niceness of them. It's how far they've come. Look at the pictures and the faces on this note..."

"I can't read it," Chantelle says, squinting at the scrunched-up note.

"That's cause it's written in Turkish, see."

I can tell she's impressed, on the verge of jealousy too, though she doesn't know why yet. Taking the note and examining it, it suits me dandy that I know she's thinking that if she ran off with it she reckons it's worth a new bike, or a proper dog house for her new mutt. But I'm so much smarter, and I know kuruş are worth hardly zilch compared to our real money.

"Well," she says, "I suppose they're...kinda cool," Pretending she's not counting with nods of the head, I can almost see the cha-ching in her eyes, like in cartoons.

The lid slams on my arm again. It's the third time and I'm getting pretty annoyed. Why's this upright part so damn heavy, I wonder. The zipped section is usually always empty. I should know. I know the nooks of Daddy's briefcase better than he does. Everything is usually thrown into the open part like he always has to leave everywhere in a hurry. It's so bulky and heavy now, I have to hold it up with both hands. What a pain. The zip isn't pulled right to the edge. Maybe there's just room for my wee finger. I give it a wee tug. Oh my, two fingers, now three, I am so naughty. Chantelle is holding the kuruş up to Mr Huxley's nose. She looks funny. And there's something in the look on her face as if she's just realised how poor she is.

The zzirrhh of the zip echoes within the cubby hole. Why does it seem louder than it actually is? If I pull it quick, it'll seem less bad. Like pulling an Elastoplast fast off your knee doesn't hurt as much as picking it bit by bit.

Done.

As the leather hinges fall forward, edges of thick glossy magazine pages flop towards me. I want to pick at their smoothness before pulling them out of their protected wee cocoon. Suddenly, Chantelle's attention has switched back to me as I swipe the magazines out and drop them on the lid of the case. The top one falls open.

"Tee-hee-hee," Chantelle sniggers. "Your Daddy is pure dead DIRTY!"

I know she's talking but her words turn to little squeaks as I sit with my bum paralysed to the ground, staring at a bunch of naked bodies doing stuff that if I turned the page at different angles I still wouldn't know which was the right way up. Chantelle grabs one end of a magazine, letting the other end flop about in the draft.

47

"Is this not just *squeak?* I mean what kind of *squeakity-squeak* have we got on our *squeaks?* Wait till I tell *squeak squeak...*about this."

I feel like strangling Chantelle and kicking Mr Huxley into the burn. My head is whizzing and I look down to find myself pounding the dirt with my fists. "Give me that..." I shout into Chantelle's face, "...and just get out!"

"Don't worry, I'm going," she says with way too big a smile. If one thing is for sure, it's that I know she knows I want to punch her. I've done it before when we were eight. But somehow, she knows I know I won't this time. Letting the magazine fall out of her hand, she winces, "Durty, durty, durty." Slowly, she gathers up all the kuruş and other bits and pieces, waving them in front of her mutt's nose. "Not so dirty, eh, Mr Hux?" She plonks my kuruş into her pocket and jingles them about a bit for effect. "I'll be seeing you, for now, Briony Marshall."

"Yeah, well tell your dad I said *hi*...if you ever see him again that is."

"WHAT-ever! And anyway, everyone knows your daddy is just an arche-lol-ogist's *assistant*..."

I watch Chantelle swagger up the garden and disappear into the close. By the end of the day, all her brothers, Becky Niven, Emma Castle, the twins Joe and Danny Greig and basically half the world will be laughing at me. My knuckles are stained brown with dirt. My nails too. I can't even bear to look at the magazines as I gather them up. But in a weird way, I've just got to have a wee peek as I flick through before shoving them back in his case. I have a good mind to just dump the briefcase right here and let Daddy sweat. Or throw it in the burn, pretending someone came into the house while he was sleeping, and stole it. Somehow, with all the choices, I find myself standing up and spitting on the briefcase, only I'm too dry and it's more like a raspberry after the third go. I lean down and wipe the grogs with my sleeve, and clean the bottom of the case of twigs and dirt. Why should *I* get into trouble? That's right, I'm not getting into bother for no one, and especially not for something Chantelle Bailey is laughing her head off over.

I race back into the close, out and past the living room window again. Mrs Carmichael is hanging about her front gate with a paintbrush in her hand. As she looks over, I stick my tongue out and sneer. I'm not even bothered what she does and have no time to hang around to find out.

I shove the briefcase behind my back, though it seems kind of stupid as it's wider than me, and not exactly disguised from the world. Poking my head round the living room door, I see Mum still watching the telly, a big meringue and a glass of misty lemonade at her side.

He is snorting and snoring away exactly how I left him. I assume Lucy is still belly to the floor with the felt tips, though I can't see her. I dash onto my knees and place the briefcase against the armchair. Just as I stand up, Lucy comes from round the side with her arms folded.

"What you doing, Briony?"

If she starts tapping her foot along with the folded arms, I think I'll scream. She looks at the briefcase for a moment, then back to me.

"Nothing! Beat it!" I whisper, too hard.

I'm pretty sure she didn't see the briefcase in my hands, but it doesn't stop her from staring at it. Just then, he gives out a long tut-tutting noise and rubs his bare arms with a little shiver.

"Well, I'm going to get Daddy a blankie," Lucy says, twisting away and losing balance with her arms still folded up to her chin.

"You do that, huh!" I say, putting my brown knuckles behind my back.

Lucy disappears like in her usual puff. One minute she's there, the next *vamoose*. Standing up straight, I round the side of the armchair. There he is. Suddenly, the image of my father, the hero...my hero has turned into MY FATHER, THE PERVERT. When I was wee, I called it "prevert," and a penis was a pelvis. Somehow that always made Elvis seem nasty. Anyway, all of a sudden why is it so hard to look at Daddy? This feeling reminds me of staring at the ugly animals at the zoo, like when I want to ignore them, but know I'm in their space and want my money's worth. His Irish Coffee and big cigar are sat by his side. Could I pour methylated spirits into his drink and stuff bird droppings into his jobby-looking thing, and watch the pain? That wouldn't even touch near the hurt I have inside me right now. I thought the spite I had for Chantelle at times was the extent of the bad feelings I could ever know. But this is something more. The very fact my teeth are grinding together tells me I have to do something before the top of my head blows off.

I can hear Mum munching away, and Lucy buzzing about in the background. They might even be talking to me, but now is not the time to answer their daft questions. Where is the key for the flammables cupboard, I wonder. That Irish Coffee is cold, but there will be another later.

I remember someone saying how fast I'll grow up when I go to the big school...well, I'm not there yet and suddenly I feel all grown up.

That's right...the key is on the hook by the clock... all I need now is the stool to reach it.

Read My Lips

Diary entry: Big-O Day -59

Who puts their bras out on the washing line when there's dreich in the air? There's only one reason her double Ds are swinging round that whirligig in October…but I'm not one to judge.

Isa's caught me at the window again muttering about how her next door can't get enough of showing off her new implants, one way or the other. Her tits would never have filled two egg cups in June, I point out.

"A woman's a woman fur aw that," Isa scoffs, half jibe, half poetic. I'm adding that to the Mockford Files, I tell her.

"Mick…" she starts, though I remind her again that's not my name now, so time to wear it out. I throw in the third person, not for the last time. "I think it's time Michaela was off up the road..." She pretends to ignore me, not for the first time.

Isa pours the tea, hastening me to sit down with that subtle jerk of her body that once seen can never be dismissed. Women do that so easily. The breathlessness of their come hither so nuanced in a way a man's sinews cannot.

I'm only here due to her having a man in. Today it's the boiler man. I ask if she'd need me in if she was expecting a boiler *lassie*. "They'll probably not have

52

the overalls to fit a lassie," she replies. And there lies the world of gender politics through the eyes of Isa McGlinchey.

"That reminds me," she says, lifting a soft yellow parcel from the chair she's now sat herself in. "I've got you a wee present. I was going to give it to you after, you know, your o-opera-tion, but I thought it…"

"It's not that Doris Day back catalogue you've been threatening me with forever?" I ask, thinking how much she struggles to spit out the Big-O. "Don't be daft," she says, taking a sip of tea. "And it's not cufflinks either." Just as well, you can't put cufflinks on a pashmina.

Isa takes her mug with her as the doorbell rings two choruses of the *Deadwood Stage*. Whenever she's got a man in I show him face and discreetly slip through to the end room. Depending on what I've chosen to wear that day, they always don that baffled, is it Arthur or Martha look. It's all very *Victor Victoria* of sorts.

Unrivalled and sat below the end room window wall is Isa's *pièce de résistance*, her off-white dressing table. Young ones nowadays would call it champagne shabby chic. But this is a dresser fit for Rita Hayworth or Betty Grable in their day.

I take my pew on the velour pink cushion stabled with its four bowly legs. Bringing the two ends of the three-way mirror towards me, I know I shouldn't, but it's like an obsession now…when Isa has a man in. I call the dresser 'the bastarding Rabbie,' as only by looking at its multiple angled reflections can I see myself as others see me. There are things a man can't hide, even when she's seated and everything is out of sight from the pelvis down. But here I am, a Glaswegian transexual with the big flat feet and an Adam's apple the shape of a Roman nose.

You know, it's not necessarily true what they say that if something looks like a duck and walks like a duck, people generally believe it is a duck. Not when it comes to a 5ft 11 gender 180° at least.

That first phone call to the gender clinic four years ago was the biggest Eureka and panic room moment of my life boiled down to one. There's many a thing the doctors, psychologists, forums and support groups never let you in on. Turning impotent is one of them.

Another was telling friends and family that I wanted to be Michaela after 39 years known and loved as Mick, a burly, fat-knuckled male of the species. This was the biggest cluster fuck of all, and the cookie crumbled with collateral damage all over the place. But folk like me are born for the challenge I suppose.

I've had as many IPL and electrolysis appointments now as I've had shouts of "There's a tranny on the bus!" The sessions go more south every visit, and nothing could've prepared me for a kindly-faced practitioner searing around my tackle, taking her from hero to Nurse Ratched.

The ding-dongs between oestrogen versus testosterone, the hot flushes, the moobs and the moods and the decisions about incisions…they are all getting me ready for the Big-O in the new year.

I'm still attempting to feminise my voice beyond

Dennistoun's Danny La Rue. It's great being a transexual in the 21st century as there's even an app for that. She's called Eva Pitch...*the wee witch*.

Isa says I should fill in the countdown by getting hooked up, popping out the aphrodisiacs and enjoying a last ride. Except she calls it "maffro-dizzyacts" so all that wisdom flies out the window. Anyway, I told her I'm sick of the meet on the discreet, curiosity piqued types.

Which reminds me, I've still got a hold of her present. The wee note attached to it reads, "Now that I've known you all these years, man and boy...and now woman xx."

Ripping open the tissue paper, it reveals a bright pink T-shirt...XL if you must. Holding it across my moobs in front of the mirror, emblazoned across the front in glitter is READ MY LIPS with a big arrow pointing down to my crotch. She really is a card is Isa.

One of her favourites, Jack Lemmon, once called Marilyn Monroe "jello on springs" when she walked past. I'm more like lard on a hard slab. But as long as I have a co-ordinated bag and eye shadow along with it, it seems to work out okay that given day.

There's one thing I do miss though, and that's Mick. There were a lot of things he didn't get to do. Like have a bromance or pee in the new urinals of The Duchess. But it's all by the by now.

The truth is I may never have a double D bra swinging from the washing line, but come the new year, I hope I'll feel a little less like the bearded lady running the gauntlet of public scrutiny out there.

Whit's the Odds?

Gully had been all enthusiastic the day he stormed into the bookies, just as Midge was about to put his last £3.50 on Limassol Lad. That was the thing about Gully, he'd knock over any loose-fitting object, and a few bolted-down ones too, on his way to reaching you and giving it the claptrap on the latest 15-watt idea buzzing about inside that thick skull of his. Midge always knew within five seconds of the rabbiting if the latest hair-brainer was worth a listen, solely in regard to the pain likely to be inflicted on his ears.

Brassic, his eyes bored into the TV screen, didn't blink from the 2.40 at Kempton as Gully threw himself onto the seat beside him. His raw, draughty momentum managed to trigger the levitation of a pile of betting slips from the table.

"Ah'm no even gonnae beat aboot the bushes wae this wan, lads," Gully said, dropping a big box with FRAGILE stamped across it onto the floor. Drizzling with intention, as fresh raindrops dripped down his Specsaver specials, he added, "efter aw, time is runnin oot as we speak."

"Hear that, Brassic," Midge said. "Nostradamus here just came fae the East wae a sign…mibbaes Ah'll jist put ma last two bob oan Apocalypse Soon. Ah hear my Limassol Lad is a donkey anywiy." Brassic remained unflinched.

Removing his thick-rimmed glasses to clean them with his tracksuit cuff, Gully said, "Naw, honestly, yous'll want tae hear this wan…"

"Here we fuckin go," Midge sighed.

"Haud oan a minute…" Brassic said, to no one in particular.

Midge and Gully followed Brassic's eyeline toward the TV commentary above.

And Lushing Lolita pips Max the Motivator by a nose at the line…Bingo Bango trails in a disappointing sixth.

Brassic, ever methodical in his cumbersome repositioning, turned to Midge and Gully. "Naw, *that's* the donkey right there," he scowled, "Bingo fuckin Bango. A cheek tae be three tae wan, an naw." Ripping his slip into four perfect quarters, even in defeat, there was no chance of an asymmetrical papery mess.

Scratching his head, as if picking a scab from it, Gully piped up, "Are you gonnae hear me oot aboot this wan or no…"

"Who's been daein yer barnet this time, Gully?" asked Bella, who was sitting on her daily perch behind the cashier counter.

"Aye," said Midge, handing a betting slip and a pile of 50 and 20 pence pieces to Bella. "You'll hiv tae tell yer Ma tae stoap using the clippers oan the Alsatian."

"You should be oan the stage at the Pavillion so ye should," Gully winced, realising the torn scab had left spots of blood behind. "Anywiy, Ah know how hard it wid be fur yous two tae drag yerselves awiy fae Glesga…but how wid yees feel aboot three months in

57

the Holland?"

"The Holland?" Brassic interrupted. "It's no callt *the* Holland, ya daft wa—"

"Ya daft windmill," stepped in Midge. "Awright then Gully, whit's happening in the Holland that wid be of any interest tae us well?"

Gully cleared his throat and took a stance of a town crier about to shout *hear ye, hear ye*. "Well, noo this wan's hot right aff the press as Ah've jist been telt it by wee Ella McClarty's niece that used tae go oot wae big Ravinder fae the cash and carry...no the wan with the big sign hangin aff the front, the other wan that's ey got discoonts oan the gairden furniture—"

"By the time he gets tae the point," Brassic said crossing arms, "the Holland will be four fuckin mile under sea level."

"Ah've been tellin ye fur years that's gonnae happen," Midge chipped in. "Result ae the melting polar ice caps."

Arms still folded, Brassic stared Midge down the eye. "Ah don't know which wan ae yees is nippin ma heid merr...him wae his double Dutch saga, or you wae yer eco-warrior heid oan."

"Well aye anywiy, wee Ella's niece..." Gully rambled on. "Ah hink it's Vicky or Wendy, or summit like that...aye anywiy, her cousin heard wind ae this recruiting agency that sends ye oot oan contracts all er Europe...well no aw ae Europe, mibbaes jist a few countries. Tae be honest, Ah heard it's jist the Holland as it stauns, but they're likely tae want tae expand any day noo..."

Cynically, Brassic asked, "And whit does this expanding agency hiv ye daein fur them exactly?"

Straightening his back like a rod, mistaking Brassic's query for enthusiasm, Gully said, "Well this is the good bit. Ye see, they gie ye the choice. Allegedly, Ella's niece's cousin is workin in a light bulb plant. But ma sources say they're lookin fur workers in a choacolate factory near Amsterdam... See, whit dae yees make ae that well?"

The stony-faced expression permanently written on Brassic's face remained as permanent as ever. "No much, tae be fair," he said, lips tight, "no much at aw."

"Here," said Midge. "Ah hope we're talkin aboot energy efficient light bulbs here?" When Gully gave a wee shoulder shrug, he asked, "So, whit's the name ae this agency?"

Without eye contact, Brassic chimed in. "Naw don't tell us, it's the Milky Bright Spark Incorporated? Or the Let There Be Light Choccy Buttons Public Limited?

Gully sank into a hunchback. "Yous should be oan stage *the gither*, so you should."

"Are ye no forgetting something here, Gully?" Midge said. "Like the last time we ventured anywhere oot ae Glesga oan wan ae your hair-brained jollies?"

Impossible not to get invested in Gully's renowned bad fortune Bella, who'd been listening in, laughed out loud. "Aw aye, is that the booze run to France that never was?"

"The very wan," Midge said.

"And why did we no get tae Calais yon day?" asked

59

Brassic.

Turning a deeper shade of crimson, Gully said, "Well it wisnae ma fault that the wee nazi jobsworth at the ferry terminal didnae understaun whit a 'piece' wis."

Brassic briefly let go of his grimace. "Aye well, you didnae exactly bend er backwards tae explain tae him that it wis a ham and pickle 'piece' that yer Maw had made up fur the trip, and no a firearm of dangerous proportions—"

"It wisnae ham and pickle," Gully said, "it wis corned dug."

"A fuckin barkin danger tae us aw, so ye urr," Midge laughed, which set Bella off too.

"And if that wisnae enough," Brassic went on, "he decides tae get it oot and show every transport polis in the vicinity the fuckin ingredients."

"Of course, Bella," Midge added, "he didnae get past takin the piece oot its container withoot us aw first gettin pounced oan by Dover's finest."

"Ye had tae be the only person still oan the planet, THE ONLY WAN," Brassic pointed, "wae an *A-Team* lunchboax fae 1985 in the shape ae a fuckin grenade!"

Gully shrugged again. "Aye, but given the fuss they were makin ye'd think Ah'd tried tae smuggle a three-day-auld corpse acroass the Channel. Wis aw a bit heavy-haunded."

"All sounds a bit *aw naw naw* than *ooh la la*," Bella laughed.

"If it's gonnae happen, it's gonnae happen tae Gully,"

Midge and Brassic said in unison.

Taking a pen to another betting slip, Brassic said, "Naw, jist you take yer money-makin tragedies tae the *Dragon's Den* and no a mile near me, son."

"Don't listen to them, Gully," winked Bella, "you could come up with Glasgow's answer to Reggae Reggae Sauce, no bother."

"Whit, Bucky Bucky Sauce?" said Midge.

"Aw, dinnae get him startit oan the inventions," Brassic said. "This is the guy that got an A-plus fae the school ae underwater hairdryers and inflatable dartboards. Wis a shame somebody had jist awready got tae Alan Sugar wae Gully's idea of a Pritt Stick butter that wan time."

"At least Ah've got a plan," Gully said, trying to hide his blushes.

Brassic wasn't for taking his foot off the throttle. "Gully," he said, "you've been runnin up and doon closes and through middens wae wan plan efter another fur years noo. But you've got merr chance ae bein hit wae Beyonce's knickers than wan ae them ever comin aff."

"Ah'll hiv yees know, Ah had nothin tae dae with that pyramid scheme in Carntyne last summer," Gully protested.

Aiming to take the heat out of Gully's cheeks, Bella sympathised, "To be fair, you've done well to build half a terrible unlucky reputation back up since."

"Wis slander so it wis," Gully said, trying to defend his red neck. "Til this day it wis slander."

"Slander?" Midge said. "We aw know it wis Brenda."

"Never did trust that lassie," Brassic said. "She ey stank ae Dettol and scampi...caustic so she wis."

Knowing he was chancing his arm, Gully said, "Aye well, we're aw allowed wan blip, in't we?"

There was an awkward silence as everyone half-looked Brassic's way.

"Awiy ye go and get aff yer soapboax, ya bampot!" Brassic said, chopping Gully down. "Ah'm awiy tae the chippie fur somethin ma belly can haunle insteed ae your nonsense up in ma lugs." He stomped out with his *don't follow me ya bam* walk, a flurry of betting slips and wafting of newspapers left in his wake.

"Thur wis nae need fur that, wis thur?" Gully whispered.

"You didnae see how much money he's loast awready the day," Midge said. "Brassic does as Brassic is."

"All the merr reason fur him tae get awiy fae the bookies," Gully said. "And escape fae Glesga awthegither, Ah'd say."

"Aye, but you say a lot ae things, Gully." Midge turned his attention to the TV screen as his Limassol Lad broke out the starting post like a prozaced turtle. "Anywiy, d'ye reckon they've no got bookies in ra Holland?"

"Aw Ah'm saying is, chances like this dinnae come alang every day, Midge. Aw ye'd need is two references and they're no even interested in yer past form."

Midge didn't know how to make it clear to Gully, without biting the top of his head off, that the only form he was interested in was the one he'd sacrificed ten Regal Kingsize and a packet of smoky bacon for.

"Well, Ah tell ye this," Gully kept on. "Ah'm aff tae write up ma references this efternoon... Ah could be wolfin doon first rate hash cookies afore the week's oot."

Glancing up, Midge saw Limassol Lad sticking to his form, making up ground among the chasing pack. "The only thing goin in your mooth will be tulips, when ye fall aff yer bike wae yer clogs still oan, and..." Just as he was about to slag Gully off some more, he looked up to see Limassol Lad just edge it by a nose at the line. "Ya fuckin dancer," he screamed. "A long shot at 18/1, that's sixty-odd smackeroonies Ah'm up!"

Gully watched on as Midge did a wee jig around their table. All their day's betting slips wafted up, while a mangled *Daily Record* and *Racing Post* flew into the air like confetti to his celebration. Pages came loose from the *Record* and landed right in front of them. Gully nudged Midge in the ribs, his gaze placed directly on the page advert that landed below their nose. EDINBURGH to AMSTERDAM — EASYJET — £49 ONE WAY.

"If that's no a sign, Midgey boy..." Gully grinned as wide as the Clyde Tunnel, "Ah dunno whit is!"

Midge picked up the page and looked closely at the print. "Mibbaes yer right fur wance, Gully, just mibbaes yer right," he smiled. "We've only wan problem, though..."

"Whit's that?"

"Brassic fuckin hates Edinburgh..."

"Aye...but he loves chocolate!"

Pulling Gully aside, so they were out of Bella's earshot, Midge said, "Another thing is, well, Ah wis gonnae ask Bella oot. And well Ah wanted tae dae it proper, me being the auld-fashioned sod that Ah am, and ye know...well noo Ah can treat her tae somewhere nice."

"Well Ah dunno if that's a good idea, Midge—"

"Ah mean it's funny, in't it?" Midge interrupted. "Here Ah'm gonnae go er there and get ma winnings which are kinda like her takings, only Ah'm hoping tae use em oan her havin a good time wae me anywiy."

"Ah'd keep yer money fur—"

"So it jist goes tae show ye whit comes aroon goes aroon, and everywan's a winner. Jesus, I'd hold my farts in for her."

Trying his best to interject, Gully said, "Aye but yer probably best jist—"

"Och, Ah know yer wantin me tae dae this Holland malarkey wae ye," Midge went on, "but well, things are all ae a sudden lookin up here, Ah'd say."

At that moment Brassic came hurtling through the door with his face tripping him. To Midge and Gully, he wore a particularly shifty demeanour than usual. Shutting the door tight, Brassic peered through the window pane as if on the look out from someone.

"Eh, and where's yer chips, Brassic?" Gully asked.

With little attention to anything but the window, Brassic replied, "Whit? Aw aye, Gino wisnae open yet."

"Looks merr like a Dempsey sandwich oan his plate,"

Midge said, almost in whisper. "A knuckle wan."

As if desperate for the toilet, Gully in his excitement crossed his legs, bopping up and down. In Midge's ear, he said, "Great moment tae bring up the aul beezer flight price, quick getaway, left the country type style, eh Midge?"

Inattentive and caught between what he wanted to ask Bella and the weirdness of Brassic's disposition, Midge said, "Aye, terrific."

Bella noticed the three-pronged shiftiness in the shop and turned to Gully first. "Are you needing to use the facilities, or what?"

"Naw hen," Gully replied, in desperation.

Handing his winning bet slip to Bella, Midge said, "He'd pish his pants before missin somethin."

"Not on my good carpet, he'll not," Bella winced. Midge looked down at the threadbare stitching of the shop's carpet and laughed louder than he should.

As Gully donned a bursting red face and a wee hop to his gait, Midge and Bella's attention turned to Brassic's hypertension. Deciding he couldn't hold his need any longer, Gully raced through the toilet door, which gave Midge a second to turn his attention solely to Bella. As he approached her counter, Brassic shouted over. "Midge, come here a minute, will ye."

"Whit? No the noo—"

"Visibly angsty, Brassic said, "Ah wid appreciate it if you wid come er here as in...*the noo*, Midge."

Torn between Bella and Brassic for a second, Midge finally crossed over to Brassic stood by the door. "Jesus, whit is it?" Midge asked. "Immaculate conception? You're merr in tune fur immaculate timing."

Brassic grabbed Midge's arm when he came close enough. "Gonnae dae us a favour..." Brassic asked.

"Whitever the question is, the answer is naw—except if yer aboot tae offer me love potion No 9."

"How much money ye got oan ye?"

"Nowt," Midge said sharpish. Ye know Ah'm skint."

Peering out the window, "Ah've jist bumped intae Danny Dempsey," Brassic said.

"No kiddin."

"Naw. And well if Ah don't come up wae three hunner and twinty quid and loose chiynge by close ae play the day, soapy bubble will come knockin. Noo, Ah've got some auld gold Ah can pawn, but it still leaves me aboot fifty-five, mibbaes sixty short, know?"

"Well ye know Ah'd like tae help ye an aw, but well Ah've no got they kinda readies at the ready."

"Ye'd be gettin me oot ae a right spot. This time the morra fuck knows whit kinda interest Danny will put oan it. He hinted oan making ma baws intae chandelier covers, the bastard."

"Like Ah say, son—"

At that second, Bella walked up to Midge holding a bundle of notes and loose change. "There ye go, Midge," she said, handing him the money. "£3.50 at 18/1 and your original bet."

Brassic and Midge shared a look that left Midge feeling decidedly sheepish. Taking the money from Bella, they walked together back to the counter. "Aye that's terrific, Bella hen," is all Midge could say, all the while feeling a relentless heavy eye from Brassic. In an attempt to keep interest in his predicament, he asked quietly, "Is it Danny Junior or Danny Senior?"

"Whit fuckin difference does it make?" Brassic said. "They're baith radio rental psychos."

"True, true..." Midge agreed. Dejectedly he counted all his new notes and handed them over to Brassic. Only the loose change found its way to his pocket. "Just don't mention chandeliers again, eh."

"All intact for the weekend now, my son," Brassic said, grabbing his testicles. "Ah tell ye whit, Ah'll even forget aboot that innocent wee play er there before." He gave Midge a soft slap on the cheek. Leaving for the door, he said, "Right then, Ah've got a date wae a Dempsey."

"At least wan ae us has got a date," Midge shrugged, just as Gully returned from the toilet looking all refreshed.

"Did ye hiv a wee word wae him then, Midge?" Gully asked. "Make him see the choccy light? Dinnae tell me...wis that him awiy tae get his passport dusted aff?"

"Naw, no exactly, Gully," Midge replied. "Reckon ye better keep that wan oan the back burner fur noo."

Gully was about to protest when Bella interrupted his thoughts. "Here, will you move that box," she said, pointing to the big cardboard carton he'd arrived with earlier. "It's a risk assessment waiting to happen."

Walking to the box, Gully turned back to Midge. "Well, we'll jist hiv tae keep workin oan Brassic then."

"Ah bloody gie up, Ah really dae," Midge sighed.

"Which reminds me," Gully went on, "Ah better go get these selt before we make tracks tae the Holland."

Totally vexed at this point, Midge said, "God gie me strength…and whit the hell's in that boax anywiy?"

"You'd better not be bringing hookey goods into my establishment," Bella shouted from the counter.

Not wanting to give Gully, his box or his delusions any more oxygen, Midge turned his attention to Bella. "How's yer Da getting oan, hen?—"

"Och it's just those blouses for Nanjid doon the market," Gully interjected.

"Shame," Bella laughed. "I was more hoping for some knocked-off Swarovskis." She turned her attention solely to Midge as he practically hung over her counter. "Ma Da's his usual daft as a brush self, thanks for asking."

Midge counted the loose change in his pocket without taking it out. He wondered if another longshot could win him back the money he'd given to Brassic, knowing he wouldn't see it again.

"I was round there for my tea last night," Bella went on. "Giving me earache he was. Asking me what the orange stuff was on the toilet seat."

Midge smiled, although felt uncomfortably confused. "Aw, right hen," he said.

"Da, I says, it's fake tan. And he said why wid ye put fake tan oan yer arse? And I says, well I would look pretty stupid with a white one. But who's gonnae see it, he said."

"Aye, who indeed?" Midge asked, regretting he'd

even asked about Bella's dad.

"You never know Da, I says. You never know."

Before he could catch himself, Midge asked, "And is yer granny still a medium?"

"Aye," Bella replied. "She is…"

Lifting a blouse from his box which got entangled with cutlery and a gravy boat, causing them to fall to the floor with a clang, Gully said, "Ye could gie her wan ae these then." Holding the blouse up for show, laughing at his own joke, "Made in China for a psychic sidekick," he said.

"Pure ignore him by the way," Midge groaned, "he's just the side-show."

As Bella shook her head in silence, Gully dropped the blouse into the box and kicked it over to a corner out of the way. Midge followed behind with purpose.

"Wid ye gie me a break here, Gully," Midge whispered loudly. "Can ye no see am tryin tae be amorous?—"

"Why don't ye try being Dugtanian fur wance?"

"Am tryin tae spin roon the charm and you're staunin there giein it butt in here and butt in there. Fur a minute Ah thought ye were gonnae tell her how this time last week ye were chuckin they blouses oot the first flair ae the cash and carry warehoose."

"While you were catchin them, ye mean?" Gully said.

"Have a day aff will ye…"

"That's whit Ah've been tryin tae tell ye, Midge. Yer no a catch…no fur Bella anywiys—"

Their conversation got cut off as Brassic walked

through the front door with a gusto about himself that wasn't around earlier.

"ALL ABOARD THAT'S GETTING ABOARD!" he shouted with a swagger.

To Midge, Gully said, "Who's put the jam back in his doughnut?"

"Yer lookin at him," Midge replied.

Crossing to the counter, Brassic smiled, "Jist a wee private joke, Bella hen."

Indulging Brassic for a moment, Bella said, "Don't tell us, a submarine from Faslane has just dropped you off at the pavement?"

"Bella, d'ye know there is a much more stylish mode of transport parked outside that door right now?" Brassic said.

From the corner, "It'll no be the Love Boat," Midge sighed dourly.

Spotting Midge and Gully huddled together in the corner, Brassic said, "Crikey, check oot these two. Midge, Ah've no seen yer face as curdled as that since Teletext ceased tae exist and yer daily fix ae Bamboozle was nae merr."

Midge shuffled back to the table in front of the counter, with Gully tailing behind. There was an awkward silence, broken by Brassic. "Midge son, if yer pretendin tae act all sore aboot earlier...well how long hiv we known each other? Since Noah was a lad, right? Anywiy, it's aw part ae the merry dance we lead callt T.A.P., eh?"

"T.A.P.?" Midge asked.

"Aye, TAP. You tap me. Ah tap you. It's oor tap

dance." More menacingly, "Besides, you'll get your bloody money back, right?" he added.

Throwing an accepting though suspicious glance, Midge said, "Uh-huh?"

"Right so whit hiv Ah missed since last in my pew?" Brassic asked, rubbing his hands together.

"Nowt, apart from the cure for cancer, and Del Boy over there flashing see-through blouses around," Bella replied playfully.

"Well well, cannae step oot ae this hotbed ae cures and action for five minutes eh?"

Gully approached the table, "Me and Midge got tae discussin some potentials fur the...ye know, nether regions?" he said.

"Did we?" Midge said, incredulously,

Brassic stood, picked up a *Racing Post* from the counter and flicked through a few pages. "Christ, we're still oan the nether regions, is it? D'ye know whit this reminds me ae, Gully? This new wacaday idea of yours, it's up there wae the time ye had an audition fur that quiz show."

"Oh aye, is that where all those pub quiz books I found in the lavvy came from?" Bella asked.

Still on the dour side, Midge said, "Aye, he hides them behind a copy ae *Penthoose* so he doesnae make himself oot tae look overly intelligent."

"Scrubbin up his general knowledge for weeks wae they books he wis, tae," Brassic added.

"Trawlin through re-runs ae *Blockbusters* and *Blankety Blank* oan YouTube and allsorts," Midge said, apparently perked up.

71

Coming to his own defence, Gully said, "It's just yer luck whit ye get asked, ye know. Bet youse dinnae know the Greek alphabet, word fur word."

"Whit use is that ye when ye struggle with the English wan?" Brassic laughed.

He took a seat at their table and adopted the image of a game show contestant. Straightening up his jumper and combing his hair across with his fingers, he rested his fidgety hands on the table. Midge snapped out of his depressive state, grabbed a bookie pen and a few betting slips and took on the role of game show host.

Reading from his first slip, Midge donned an affected Kelvinside accent. "And our next contestant is James Gulliver from Upper Springburn. Is that near Lilliput, James?"

With a stern wink, Brassic warned, "Watch it, Wogan!"

Gully crossed over to read the betting slip in Midge's hand in a state of confusion, thinking it genuinely *did have* his details written on it.

"Now a starter for ten, just ease you in nicely..." Midge said, clearing his throat.

"Fire away, son." Brassic gave a quick *faux* smile to his audience.

"The food and drink round...now, what is a mixture of avocado, chilli and lime juice commonly known as?"

"Eh...Guatemala?" Brassic replied.

"Hmm, not quite," said Midge. "Perhaps geography is more your strong point, hmm? Let's see, how's about this. The Benelux countries consists of Belgium,

Luxembourg and which other nation?"

"Oh now…is it Wales?"

"Well, not quite," Midge said, still laying the Kelvinside on thick. "A bit of a natural world lover though are we? Let's see if this one is more on your radar. Now, if you were superstitious, which black and white bird would you salute if you were to see it alone?"

"Aw that wan's easy…" Brassic jumped up. "Ah just watched *Happy Feet* the other night as well…"

"Awright, awright…" Gully shouted, louder than he realised.

Back in his own voice and realising Bella was leaning over her counter highly entertained, Midge said, "So he gets past the first round ae preliminary auditions—"

"Fuck knows how—" muttered Brassic.

"And intae a simulation set up at the STV studios," Midge explained. "Met Nicky Campbell and allsorts, didn't ye?"

"He wis a very nice man," Gully said, defensively.

"Spun the wheel fur him tae, eh?" Midge reminded.

"Aye."

"Even got a free spin token, an aw?"

"Ah did."

"And whit did happen tae that free spin token?"

"It kinda, eh…off the…and went over…and…" Gully mumbled.

"It went fuckin skitein aff the wheel and through the air frisbee style," announced Brassic. "Takin wae it wan ae they autocues and ten grand worth ae camera

73

lens wae it."

"It didn't..." said Bella.

"It did," Midge confirmed. "If they were filmin Contestants Dae the Funniest Things ye wid've had merr chance ae getting yer mush oan telly."

"Christ, you're right," Bella said, "it could only happen to Gully. No divine intervention that day?"

"Merr hope ae Sydney Devine intervening wae Gully than…him up there," Brassic said pointing upward.

"Ah'll have yees know," Gully said, trying to down heat. "Ah've had many an unexplained miracle and spiritual moment."

"Whit, aw they times tears fell doon the face ae yer Auntie Mamie's Virgin Mary when you were in her hoose?" Brassic laughed. "Took them three years tae figure oot it wis an overflowing watter pipe fae the loft. Ye only visited her when it wis raining, comin in fae playin in the park acroass the road."

"Slipped aff the tongue at the time though..." Midge recalled, putting his hand up as if he were reading a sign above. "The Springburn Messiah, aged 13¾."

"Aye but whit aboot the time Ah managed tae sell aw they tea towels and oven mitts wae the Pope oan them," Gully said. "Ah guess some folk don't mind his holiness huvin a burnt napper wiping the crap aff their kitchen coonters."

"D'ye know, Bella," Brassic sighed, "there's parts ae China where they don't believe in rubbish tips, so they just send all the shite tae him." He stood up and handed Midge a fiver. "Here, awiy doon the chippy wae this. Gie me some peace tae follow ma form," he said, grabbing a tattered *Racing Post*.

"This'll be a donation toward my T.A.P. fund then eh?" Midge said, pocketing the note. He didn't hang around for Brassic's reply. "Gully, you comin?" he asked, reaching the door.

Distracted by his own thoughts, "Eh? Naw, yer awright Midge," Gully said. "Ah've just thought ae something Ah need tae dae first."

"Please yerself." To Bella, Midge shouted, "If Brassic gies ye any trouble just whistle *Scotland the Brave* as yer S.O.S."

"Dinnae choke oan yer pizza crunch, son," Brassic called back as Midge and Gully stepped out.

Brassic made a beeline for Bella. "Ah want ye tae keep this tae yerself, hen," he said, slipping a bundle of £20 notes and a betting slip across the counter. "300 oan Ship's Mate tae win the 2.20 at Newmarket." Looking over his shoulder while Bella counted the notes, he pocketed the completed bet slip in swift motion.

"I'm here not to ask nor answer," Bella said, stiffly.

"Good lassie," Brassic said, a bit on the patronising side. He looked at his slip, holding it up excitedly. Ship's Mate, am trusting ye tae bring hame the bacon fur me the day."

"All aboard, who's coming aboard?" asked Bella.

"That's it, hen," Brassic said, turning to leave. "Ah'll be back before ma boat comes in…"

Later the same afternoon while the bookies was empty

and Bella was sorting her paperwork, Gully peeked his head around the door. Seeing that no one was around he burst through, looking shiftily behind. As he approached the counter, Bella noticed him carrying another box, although smaller than the one earlier.

"Ah fancy a wee flutter the day," Gully announced.

Genuinely surprised, Bella said, "Strike me down. In all the time you've been coming in here, you've broken the lavvy chain twice, been off with numerous amounts of my pens, blocked the doorway with yer junk...but never have you crossed my palm with coin."

"Och naw, Bella. Sometimes it's just a feelin Ah get noo and again," Gully smiled. "A feelin in ma watters. Wance in a blue moon is enough tae be goin oan wae." He wrote out a bet slip and pocketed the pen. "There ye go, 2.20 at Newmarket, Hot Rod Rosie tae win oan the nose."

Bella took the slip as Gully reached down to take the money from his shoe. As she turned her back for a second she couldn't see the bended down Gully. As he popped back up she got a surprise and he gave an even bigger one when he handed a wad of cash over to the tune of £180. "This race is proving popular today," she said.

"Ye don't say," Gully replied, a bit too sly. "Mind no let it slip that ye seen me dae this, okay?"

"What is this today, the betting confidential?" Bella said. "You lot are acting weirder than usual and that's truly saying something."

"It's an opportunist's day, Bella. They're special kinda days. In many ways Ah've been waiting a long time fur this day tae come…"

As Midge and Brassic entered the shop, Gully moved away from the counter sharply.

"Here," Brassic said. "Ah dae my bit fur the environment…"

"Ah'm jist saying," Midge sighed, "carryin a triple pack ae Lynx Africa aerosols hame fae Superdrug withoot the aid ae a polybag is no a definition ae daein yer bit fur the environment."

"Away and fuck off wae that bag fur life rant ae yours," said Brassic. "Yer like the fuckin recyclin Gestapo." To Gully and Bella, he said, "Last week he found two 3-litre White Lightning plastic empties in the glass bin and blew a gasket. Ah said, the wee jakey that drank them had probably fell in the bin wae them, case closed."

"Ye don't get it dae ye?" Midge said, jumping on his proverbial soapbox. "We don't own this bloody planet. We're jist lease hauders. It's a duty tae maintain oor world. But whit are we doin eh? Suffocatin it wae carbon monoxide, causin the polar ice caps tae melt. It willnae be that when the oceans rise and the Clyde floods over. It won't be that when manky watter comes floodin up the Clyde Tunnel and the Calton and Glesga Green are submerged forever."

"That'll be handy for us though, eh?" Brassic shrugged.

"How d'ye work that oot?" asked Midge.

"Well, when we come tae rent oot oor high rises in Springburn, we can advertise them as having sea views…"

Gully sat at the table. "Jesus, is he oan aboot they shifting continental shelves again?" he asked.

Taking a seat across from Gully, Brassic replied, "Aye, and that usually only spells wan thing."

"Whit's that?"

"He's no had a bit for months."

A tense silence fell as Midge threw Brassic a heavy, intense stare. Bella came from behind her counter to tidy up the strewn betting slips and tattered newspapers. Unaware of the conversation just gone before, she broke the silence. "What's up with your faces?"

"Midge hisnae had a bit fur months," Gully said.

Rattled, Midge flew across the table for Gully's throat. "Ah swear to God, Ah'm gonnae—"

Brassic intervened just in time and put his face up to Midge. "Noo noo, that wid be pure sacrilege seeing as you're an environmentalist, son. Eco-warriors dinnae dae violent."

Aiming to soothe the situation, Bella said, "Midge is right though. It helps to be at one with mother nature. I believe if you want something you just shout it, shout it out to the universe."

"Whit, so if Midge shouts out that he wants his hole the night," Gully said, "she'll see him right?"

Trying to keep calm with Bella so close, Midge groaned, "Hiv you came aff yer medication the day just fur a wind up?"

"Environmental doesnae work well in a recession though," said Brassic. "Ah'm tellin ye, see in the boom times, folk wid throw oot stuff ye could always recycle."

"That you could sell on, you mean?" Bella joked.

"Wan man's junk tossed in a skip wis another man's cooncil tax paid fur two months," Brassic continued. "Last week Ah wis oan that Freecycle website… and whit did Ah see? A gairden trug, whitever the fuck that is, an insect catcher tube, 15 jam jars, three waw tiles and some auld cunt lookin tae rehame his cockerel. That troops is the fuckin sign ae oor times."

"Aye, it's awright fur him tae hiv a rant," Gully said, to no one in particular.

"Whit wis that?" Brassic snapped.

"Ah wis jist sayin…" Gully backtracked. "Ah'm sure Bella would love a cock aboot the place."

"I think you'll find that's the last thing I need," Bella said, before walking back behind her counter. Once there she shared a wink with Gully.

Throwing a suspicious dagger at Gully, Midge said, "Here whit you up tae? Ah seen ye giein Bella the eye there."

"Ah wisnae, Midge. Honest," Gully protested. He stood abruptly. "Ah wouldnae dae that, specially wae Bella cos ae—"

"Here, whit's that smell?" Brassic interrupted. All eyes turned to Gully. "Whit the fuck's in that boax?"

"Och it's just a couple ae trout."

"Aw you've no been buyin muck affy wee Shughey McFadden have ye?" Brassic said. He wafted his hand about his nose. "The fish he sells is truly feral."

"Who's Shughey McFadden when he's at hame?" asked Midge.

"He's that wee fella wae the limp and the googly

79

eyebaws," Brassic said. "Merr slippery than the guppies he flogs. He goes aroon the fancy hotels tryin tae sell the Yanks and the Japs aw the salmon, sayin it's just oot the Clyde."

"And whit *you* daein wae it, Gully?" Midge asked.

"Dae yees no watch the papers or read the news?" Gully said, as if on the tip of one of his sales pitches. "They're aw tellin us we need merr oily fish and less sausage suppers. It's the latest thing, that Omega 3. Gettin a bit three times a week can put ten years oantae yer lifespan."

"Ha!" Brassic snapped. "Well in Springburn's case another ten year makes sixty-four plus injury time."

"Ah think Ah'd rather keel er noo than eat whitever the fuck's in that boax," Midge said, boaking.

"See under aw the stoor and chip fat there's a Glesga wantin tae be healthy," Gully went on. "Aw they folk going tae the gym before their work at hauf six in the mornin…well there's yer market there, see?"

"Aye, a meat market ae manky sweatin flesh by the time you'd get yer hawns on them," Midge smirked.

"There's a kind ae folk that want tae eat well, live healthy and better themselves," Gully kept on. "Hard tae believe, Ah know."

"Aye, but see there's wan thing you'll no get awiy wae in Glesga," Brassic said. "And that's folk gettin ideas above their station. Do ye no remember whit happened tae Sheena Easton efter she went away tae America and came back wae that aw affected Lulu accent? She played Glesga Green and came within an inch ae the infirmary."

"That was wan good use ae a ginger boatle," Midge laughed.

"So ye see, Gully…" Brassic said, as if wanting to bring proceedings to a close. "Yer no impressin anywan."

"Listen, am no wanting tae eat the wares ae Shughey McFadden," Gully said. "Am jist interested in gettin intae the minds ae the folk that dae. Like Ah say, it's an Omega 3 thing. You've got tae get inside the psychology ae yer punter."

"Jesus, Ah've heard it aw noo," said Brassic. "You've been watching too many ae they *Horizon* documentaries fur yer ain good."

"There is a whole world oot there, lads." Gully started to soapbox. "A world, that if ye were tae staun and look at it, would make Glesga look like the maist insignificant place in the world. Cause let's face it, we feel like the maist insignificant people in the world maist ae the time."

"Whit…" Brassic cut in. "And goin tae work in a choacolate factory in Holland is gonnae help you better yerself?"

"Aye by the wiy, Ah've since done ma research and this is quality choacolate Ah'd be dealin wae," Gully said proudly. "Nane ae yer Flakes and Caramacs we're talkin aboot here."

"And Ah suppose you've got a Jackie Chan wae aw this choacolate?" Midge asked, half mock, half curious.

"Ae course Ah've got a plan," Gully replied. "Dae ye know how much a minted choacolate liqueur wid set ye back these days?"

"Cannae say Ah dae, naw," said Midge.

"Put it this wiy, if Ah got ma hawns oan just a few cases ae they liqueurs," Gully said, pointing at his fishy box. "It wid make the return oan six ae Shughey McFadden's trouts look like small fry."

"Whit, are ye gonnae flog them doon the Amsterdam canals oan a pedalo?" Brassic laughed. "Or take them acroass the German border and sell them next tae the sauerkraut?"

"Naw, am gonna import them back intae Scotland," Gully replied, dead set serious.

"Aw, Ah've heard it aw noo," said Brassic, turning his back.

"Jist a matter of logistics is aw," Gully smiled.

"Here, Gully," said Midge, "ye better avoid Calais as yer thoroughfare. You'll no want tae get done again fur a piece and hot choacolate this time."

Midge and Brassic shared a mocking laugh.

"As I see it," Bella chipped in casually, "he's still the only one around here with a bit of gumption. At least he has a go, even in the lean times." She pointed at Gully as Midge and Brassic looked on in subdued shock. "That one sees the world for what it is, and adapts accordingly."

With his nose all out of joint, "Well here, Ah don't know aboot that," Midge said.

"You two just sit about slagging anything that moves," Bella went on. "You are all hiding from something or somebody, at least with him it's harder to hit a moving target."

Gully sat up straight, all chuffed with himself.

"Aw aye," Brassic snapped. "The aw-Glaswegian hero. Gully, you'll hiv tae look up *accordingly* in wan ae yer quiz books."

"See," Gully said, as he walked tall over to his box and lifted it up to the chest. "Bella's right. Ye think Ah've no got hopes and dreams? Ah reckon some cunts just look at us and think, whit a bunch ae nae hopers. It's a Glesga thing, cos folk oan the ootside think that's whit we've got the least ae. Well, that's the wan thing Ah haud ontae the maist...ma dreams." He attempted to walk casually through the door, but not before ungainly fumbling the handle with the box between his arms.

Unfazed, Brassic said, "Och, we know yer just joshin aboot, Bella."

"Am I now?" Bella said with shade.

"Aye Brassic," Midge said. "How did ye get on with that joab interview?"

"Whit joab interview?" Brassic groaned. "Ah didnae even get a joab application."

"And why did ye no get an interview, an application, or a sniff ur a whiff?"

"Somethin tae dae wae the fact there's nane of the above in that world oot there that Bella reckons Gully's got such a good handle oan."

"Jesus, it's not a violin I can hear," Bella said, "it's the world's biggest pity party."

"He's right though, Bella," Midge said softly. "This city has gone tae the dugs. It's only the pound shoaps, Cash Convertors and turf accountants like yerself that dae a rerr trade these days."

Bella folded her arms waiting for more laments. Brassic obliged. "You tell me whit's oot there Bella, hen? Jesus, ye cannae even make money fae knocked aff fags anymerr such is this world we live in noo. Ah mind the days Ah could flog a two hunner pack ae woodchips and toe nails doon the Barras fur a seller's price. Noo folk are hit er the heid by whit's right and whit's wrang. It's aw Watchdug and the man fae the Trading Standards sayin NAW!"

"I see, yes. What's the world comin to when the common or garden hustler can't make a buck anymore?" Bella said. "Even in the good times, knocked-off fags and booze never kept you afloat."

"Christ, is this the wiy it's gonnae be?" Brassic said. "Come intae the bookies fur a punt and walk oot wae a lecture in tow?"

"What about you, Midge?" Bella asked. "Why do you not take up the chance of this gig in Amsterdam? Sounds a bit of a no-brainer to me."

"The day Ah get involved in another frolic fae the bollock will be—" Brassic cut in.

"Whit aboot me, Bella?" asked Midge.

"If you're lookin tae Midge tae chiynge the economy yer lookin in the wrang place," Brassic said. "Save a tree or write a love poem, aye. But he's nae Alan Sugar."

"Fuck off," Midge snapped. "Yer no exactly Rockefeller yerself. At least Ah've got a romantic bone in this here boady. Your idea ae romance is a Gino's Special and a gettin her legless fae the waist doon oan Mad Dog."

Gully stepped back into the shop, free from carrying his box of wares. It was five minutes til the off for the 2.20 at Newmarket and he didn't want to miss his hopes pinned on Hot Rod Rosie. "Awright Bella hen," he said, with a wink and a wee hop.

"Ah swear tae Jesus, if this is your attempt at flirting wae Bella again—" Midge said, trying to keep his voice low, but seething inside.

"Naw Midge, it's no like that. Ah wis—"

"Thieving yer best pal's potential bird is it..." Brassic said. "Noo that is sacrilege."

"Eh, Ah don't think that coonts," Gully protested. "*Potential* isnae the word Ah'd be using—"

"Whit's stoappin ye anywiy, Midge?" Brassic egged on. "You leave it too late and the Calton really will be under as much watter as his fuckin Holland."

"Aye, Ah know, Ah know," Midge said, feeling his palms going sweaty. "Ah'm jist waitin fur the right moment."

"Ah mean..." said Brassic, "ye don't want tae be haudin aff and the next thing ye know it's like a scene fae Titanic and she's floating doon wan side ae the Clyde oan a mantelpiece and you're driftin doon the ither wiy on yer meltin polar ice cap wae a handcuff stuck tae yer wrist."

"Midge...Midge," Gully attempted. "There's summit ye should—"

"CARPE DIEM, ma man!" Brassic egged on. "Carpe fuckin Diem!"

"Yer right," Midge said, standing with real purpose.

"Yer fuckin right. Ah'm gonnae dae it, and Ah'm gonnae dae it the day..."

Commentary of the next race became audible from the TV screen above Bella's counter.

Next up on the card is the 2.20 from Newmarket, the Maiden Fillies' Stakes. As the eight runners and riders approach the stalls, the clear odds on favourite for this mile and six-furlong race is Ship's Mate...

Breathing in and out deeply, Midge announced, "In fact, Ah'm gonnae dae it noo..."

Brassic ignored Midge's moment of epiphany, more interested in his view of the upcoming race and his Ship's Mate wager. Gully made a wry smile in Brassic's direction and shook his head. As Brassic stood animated, eyes focused on the screen, Gully remained calmly seated.

Midge tentatively approached the counter, his palms clammy with nerves. "Eh, Bella hen," he said. "Have ye got a minute?"

Bella stopped busying herself behind the counter. "Aw for you, Midge, I've got almost two."

And they're off...Trixie Doll makes a good start on the firm ground, hotly followed by Ship's Mate and the pack...

Taking a deep breath, Midge asked, "Well, Ah wis just wonderin whit ye were daein oan Thursday night?"

"Well...I'm usually a bit wet on a Thursday night," Bella said.

"Aw right," Midge replied. Baffled, he asked, "Eh?"

"I go to the swimming—"

Last Laugh sticks tightly to the rail coming round the

bend at halfway as Ship's Mate looks comfortable and lets the pack pick up the pace...

"Aye, I go on a Thursday as it's the late closing session," Bella said. "Sometimes fit in a massage and the sauna too."

His nervousness having upped a notch, Midge said, "Aye, well that clearly aw keeps ye, eh, trim and that. You'll never be a big Bella...eh, Ah mean big, Bella."

"True, true," Bella said. "Best form of exercise there is."

"Aye, so they say, hen. So they say."

Coming now into the straight and it's Ship's Mate looking strong. Trixie Doll and Last Laugh hold firm with no signs of lacking pace as the trailing pack start to fall away.

With sweat beads starting to glow on his forehead, Midge asked, "So eh, would ye be busy the following night at aw?"

"What's that, the Friday? Well aye, Friday night is poker night. Set in stone for the last, oh Christ, five years now."

"And Ah suppose yer helluva busy oan a Saturday evenin an aw, eh?"

"No, not really," Bella gave.

There's no let up in stride in the final furlongs between this trio as Last Laugh sticks to the rail looking for a way to edge the inside line.

All perked up, Midge said, "Aw right, well—"

"Saturday nights are all about a curry and a bottle of wine...and snugglin up on the sofa with Denise."

"Awww, is that yer dug?"

"Eh, no...Denise is my girlfriend."

With total redneck shock, "Yer girlfr—" Midge said. "Well eh, aye ae course she's eh no a dug, Ah mean eh, like a dug..." He backed away awkwardly from the counter bumping into the table.

Gully stood as if to catch Midge before he lost his footing. "That's whit Ah've been tryin tae tell ye," he said. "Ye were ontae plums wae Bella..."

"Aye, no fuckin kiddin," Midge winced, not knowing where to put himself.

"Midge, Bella bats wae the other baw," Gully went on.

"Well Ah know that noo, don't Ah," groaned Midge. "Fur fuck's sake."

Last Laugh appears penned into the rail by Ship's Mate. In the penultimate furlong, it's Ship's Mate who's certainly looking the stronger though Trixie Doll holds the pace...

"Keep the perfume fur yer Ma," Gully said, as he turned his attention to the race.

"Aye, Ah get it. She's a bean, a dyke, a rug muncher. Why the fuck did ye no tell me?"

"Ah've been tryin tae tell ye fur ages—"

"Ye forgot muff diver..." Brassic chimed in, his eyes entranced by the race on the screen.

"Did you know aboot this?" Midge said, angrily. "Ye did, didn't ye? You knew all alang and even encouraged me knowin Ah wis goin in kamikaze. Some fuckin mate you urr."

Midge walked over to Brassic with a clenched fist, while Gully and Brassic fought for a space in front of the TV screen, both hyped with tunnel vision.

Last Laugh appears to have lost her last furlong legs, leaving it a two-horse finale between Ship's Mate and Trixie Doll…

"Och you've always went efter the wrang wans, Midge," Brassic said, unaware that Midge was ready to throw a punch. "Been daein it aw yer days. Wimmin don't want poems and roses and…c'moan Ship's Mate, ya wee dancer. Get the whip oot, fur fuck's sake."

Futilely trying to keep a resemblance of calm about himself, Gully shouted, "Oooh, aye, mon, giddy up."

Brassic threw a quizzical look at Gully. Midge kept his eyes fully on Brassic. Gully's stare was caught on something on the left of the TV screen.

"Awright, enlighten us then, Brassic." Midge was near foaming at the mouth. "Whit dae wimmin want, eh? Whit is it they're really efter…a *real* man like you?"

With his eyes unmoved from the screen, Brassic said, "You're beyond enlightenin, son. Yer like Buzz fuckin Lightyear. Tae infinity and past beyond with whit you'll ever know aboot wimmin."

And they're neck and neck on the final run in, there's absolutely nothing to pick between Ship's Mate and Trixie Doll… And it looks like Ship's Mate has just enough to make a final surge...

"Come on ya wee beauty. Come tae daddy…" Brassic had the first sign of excitement seen on his face for weeks.

"Is that whit ye said tae Roxy?" Midge asked. Gully switched from the screen to Midge with a look of incredulous fear.

For a moment, it appeared as though Brassic hadn't heard Midge's words. "C'mon Ship's Matey, c'mon and give me a big fuckin bumper packet," Brassic screamed. "Look she's gonnae romp it. Haha, Trixie Doll my erse…"

And it looks like Ship's Mate has just enough to hold on…OH AND SHE'S DOWN! Ship's Mate has lost her footing with inches to go to the line, unseating her rider as he lands over the line before her.

"Well wis it?" Midge said. "Is that whit ye said tae Roxy before you put yer fists intae her kidneys that time?"

Brassic heard Midge this time.

Gully looked back to the TV screen…

And it's Red Hot Rosie avoiding a collision with Ship's Mate and Trixie Doll who crosses the line intact to take the Maiden Fillies' Stakes.

…his eyes as big as Dutch chocolate liqueurs.

Organic Loins

They met at Queen's Park farmers' market
She, third generation Strathbungo,
twice wed—He, Albert Drive hipster,
shouldering a wee WWF tote bag

Talked about loving local,
all the while radiating low
carbon footprint pride

She said her veg patch
was bumper this summer,
he replied his window box
had a lot to answer for

Her female wiles wanted
pinned against that box ledge,
his flanks hankered to bump
her patch up close

They walked opposite ways,
eyes full on dilated
—only a fortnight
til the next farmers' market

Vincenzo

Mind that day it was blowin a hooley
and you came down the street
roller-skated up,
like a couple
of Ford Cosworths
were stuck to your ankles?

Evel Knievel style
you jumped
the McJimpsey's hedge
like it was diddly
and the dug in the garden
didn't know if it was
Christmas or Cumbernauld,
a mirage or the Mujahideen

A boy named Vincenzo
was always going to stick out
—a wild Neapolitan heart from your da
though more pan loaf
on your mother's side

They said a candle so bright
couldn't burn
for too long,
but Vinnie my boy
nothing was for drubbing
you out in your heyday

A mere bagatelle on the streets
you were not,
making yourself a name
where grown men wouldn't cross you
due to mafioso rumours
and ties to ice cream wars

Donned in Diadora B-Elites and Fila trackies
like they were street Versace
you rolled Royston into a joint,
inhaled Maryhill
and puffed out Partick
all in a day's graft

That azzurro Vespa saw legit
hookey goods fall off its back,
as you could flog dead fish
from South China seas
as long as it bore
an Isle of Capri stamp

By the time you turned a man
you were a mile wide and an inch deep,
a few Glasgow smiles given to rival cheeks
over the lassie from Cadder
who born your wild seed

But no one and nothing could catch you
Vinnie my boy,
like a poly poke on an October day

you slipped over the rooftops
and up the backroads til the heat melted

Then one day the whispers at the bus stops,
The wee Aye-Tie hasn't been seen for three week
Word had it you'd washed up on Speirs Wharf
with a catfish in each pocket,
or better still
scat back to your tribe
in old Napol*ee*

Sugartown

Oh Glasgow,
you've gone and done it now
Ripped me ruin
and cast asunder

Your diesel belly-ed potholes,
slick dreich of pavement and
urban surge renewed,
top to bottom you
give me life and suck the gasp
from my lungs in that unbroken
devastating perpetualness

Like the top coat of Saturn's rings am
bound to your crust by Isaac's gravity
Never can I fall,
for winching from you is like tailspinning
into the ether, the abyss
or something wholly sicker

Oh Glasgow,
aye pal, you've gone
and done it now,
wee, beautiful sweet shite that you are

My Unrequited Debut, and You

Whoever it was that said, *the worst way to miss someone is to be sitting right beside them knowing you can never have them* got it spot on. That's the way it was with me. Me sitting aside you. Only in French study class was my handwriting so neat and tidy, because you complimented it so. How I wanted to return that insignificance—on your part— a hundredfold, to unguard my approval of the shallowest inhale of your body, in rest and motion.

You never noticed how I'd deliberately sit to your right, me being left-handed, you being right—that way our elbows inadvertently brushed against each other as we copied past participles from brown-papered textbooks. The layers of school blouse and polyester cardigan were a thin veil to the rush those gentle grazes swept through me.

All these years later you'd think I wouldn't stop dead still at the sight of green gingham, and upon hearing The Buzzcocks' *Ever Fallen In Love with Someone*. At sixteen, perhaps I hoped I'd *never* stop dead in my tracks at the sight of green gingham, and in the distance *in love with someone you shouldn't have fallen in love with*. As now, if I do, that piece of you I've kept buried in a catacomb of retention will have ceased to jar. But I don't want it to.

It was an Indian summer, that autumn in fifth form,

when you first glided into Monday morning assembly. You, falling on my eyes like the freshest leaf spun in a breeze, cast from the tallest tree. My adolescent heart so unready, yet supple it was to composing a rapture—a rapture at liberty to immerse every morsel of me to its core. They don't teach you that as part of the syllabus. Not that feeling. Nope. No warning nor subsequent guidance given to that sensation which starts life as a held sideways glance, mysteriously morphing into a monomaniacal force.

Wispy little strands from hair so long and curly and as dark as two in the morning fell gently on your shoulder, as I found myself two rows behind in French class. I sat mesmerised by the way you'd twist a mass of locks—so beautifully unkempt—secure with only the aid of a pencil, unveiling a neck so soft and radiantly sallow. Mapping your face at every turn, is something I'd do countless times, always alighting my gaze on lips innately peachy, glistening from the balm you'd apply at the start of every lesson. When we sat in a circle for group oral, I'd shuffle my glares from you to the blackboard, you to the door, back to you via the ceiling, and all over again, displaying a round of optical gymnastics for the besotted.

And you strolled everywhere, never in a hurry, effortlessly on time for everything. I was the one red and flustered endlessly rushing late into French class. Perhaps it was my subconscious effort to make you notice me. You can't miss the one stumbling over tables, secreting nervous perspiration onto plywood desktops. All I got for my troubles was a succession of

97

warnings and a hundred Gallic lines. I was never in bother with teachers before that term, so I guess whoever penned *The Things We Do for Love* was on the money too.

Your alluring mystery—it was this very essence of your difference that intrigued me and every snippet I gained of you reeled me in tighter and tighter. And beyond that, it was the front of sheer indifference to how you stood apart that kept me absorbed. And there was the likes of me—not that anyone seemed like me. I'm sure I wasn't on anyone else's mental list. Nondescript, shifting through corridors so as to keep attention away from everyone and everything. And there was you. Yet, you were like the girl with no past and no history. Where had you come from? I could tell you preferred to keep yourself undisclosed. I tapped into that. For I played the same game, and this became the common ground that acted as my stepping stone.

By the time that balmy autumn had given way to the eventual cold snap, I was adrift from all worldly events. So rapt I was in you that waiting entire weekends for Monday morning French class was longer than the thought of six weeks in Science detention with old Willoughby breathing down my neck.

Then came the day that made it possible for an angry young cynic to turn believer, that there was someone up there answering prayers. Near to prelim exams, our French ma'am, Mrs Tait announced, "Any pupil who feels they require additional language sessions may book set time blocks with the use of this classroom…" I knew I needed extra French study, as I had such a hard time concentrating with your presence sandwiched between my desk and the flow of Taitster's trills and warbles. "…Those who wish to sign up, remain behind at the end of this morning's lesson."

I watched as the peely wallies loped out of the classroom in record time, nearly falling over themselves in the process. As Taitster wiped the remains of *aujourd'hui c'est lundi le 16 novembre* from the board, I counted the bodies out the door until the room was left with two volunteers. You swivelled round, perhaps in anticipation of the chance you'd have Taitster's domain to study alone in. And I sat there, almost too afraid to look up in case your face was etched with disappointment at the sight of your prospective "study buddy." Bravely, I lifted my eyes to see your gaze softly drift around the room and finally fall on me as a snowflake falls on a wilted leaf. It was then, as I was caught suspended in a moment combined of two missed heartbeats and a fleeting bout of dry mouth, that those peachy lips gave a little upturn of approval.

At break, before our first study period, I stood in front of the bathroom mirror pleading with myself, *don't be a bumbling idiot, don't be a bumbling idiot*, saying it repeatedly until caught and overheard by another pupil, subsequently falling into my usual catatonic stupor. If you remember, I was painfully shy back then, and I'd have forgone a vital organ to be injected with a spun of witticisms and anecdotes to have you falling off your chair with laughter. Instead, of course, I entered timid and awkwardly. You'd chosen the last table of the middle aisle, the only two desks on which warm rays shone through the window onto your back if caught in the mid-morning sun.

You introduced yourself perfunctorily. I laughed within. As if I didn't know your name. *How ridiculous.* And then I immediately reprimanded myself for silently suggesting you were ridiculous. Oh Christ, I knew I was really in trouble. I took my seat beside you and spent the next forty minutes inhaling a sweet, musky scent that seemed to fill the air within two square feet of your solemn *joie de vivre*. I scrutinised your small, sallow and perfectly shaped hands, the healthy whiteness of your nails and the flawless sparkle of your teeth. I'd never felt so peely wally in all my life, but in those moments it felt breathtaking to bask in the aroma and light of your exotic and mysterious beauty.

Monday mid-mornings and Thursdays after school became the blissful little structures of my week. I treated them like occasions in which everything I did outside the cocoon of our study class seemed prosaic.

"My brother is at university," you shared, as I copied a row of complex verbs from a textbook.

"My brother isn't," I said, wishing to bugger he was, if only to assign a sliver of valid mutuality between us.

"You're into sports, aren't you?" you asked. "I split my shorts one time at my old school, doing a gymnastics routine. Swore I'd never do sports again."

"Maybe it was the shorts and not your roly-poly ability?" I said, too offhand by far. You smiled and applauded the calligraphy of my Fs and Qs.

"Well, you know," your face had became suddenly sober and challenged, "I'm expected to go too."

"To uni?" rhetorically I asked, embarrassed by the possibility we were still on the subject of gymnastics.

"Uh-huh," you gave quietly, those top pearlies all the time biting into the moistness of your bottom lip.

Hesitantly I probed, "And you don't want to?"

"Of course I do. What else would there be? My mother and my father both did, and now Warren. Last night my mother assured me a family like ours should sit on a four-legged chair not a three-legged stool, or something like that."

"A family like yours?"

"Yes, a Jewish family."

A Jewish family? That was it. That was like the crux of your difference, aesthetically, characteristically, morally. I'd never known a Jewish person before, or at least, if you know what I mean, *known* they were Jewish, hence the shekel hadn't dropped.

My recognition of Judaism was diminutive, almost completely ignorant up to that point. A meek under-standing of The Holocaust and an opinion of apparent cruelty involved in the act of circumcision was about my breadth of it. In a moment of clarity, I realised it was also this that kept you withheld. In our institution, which fell short of an abundance of broad-mindedness and liberality due to a kind of social and geographical default, I considered how daunting it must've been to bring attention to a religion that was so misunderstood in our environment—my docile insight of it being a case in point.

Only with me did you share, in tacit confidence, this principal part of you. Perhaps you underestimated the peely wallies. Perhaps I did too in my eagerness to disassociate myself from them. At that age, no one wants to be different. We may, deep down, want to embrace the thing that makes us different. But *I knew* what it was like to feel solitary in something, and to choose the easy option—to cower away under a blanket of undetected breath rather than face a salvo of name-calling fused with peer ostracism. Deciding it's better to feel ostracised in silence than in resonance wasn't a tough decision to make.

You spoke at times about your mother and father—their education, their social standing, their separation. You curiously spoke of them as if they remained together, or at least together in the sense of their shared responsibility in steering you toward university. "It's alright for some," you said, "there's no one putting pressure on you to excel. If you made it, then great, even if you were punching above your weight. If you didn't, who'd be disappointed...? You don't carry that expectation on your shoulders."

You were right though. A forthcoming life of academia wasn't my burden. I had this other demon to deal with. A torment that was wrapped up in the intensity of my feelings for you. Ironically, every extract of the fear and loathing you fed onto me brought us closer, and closer. It was then I wished the world would disappear in a sudden armageddon, you and me and Taitster's classroom the only tangible things left in the desolation.

Not long after, you introduced me to your lunch buddy in the corridor. As if I didn't know *his* name. Now that was ridiculous. By this stage, I knew his name along with an inventory of other little data-mined morsels—where you lived, what your phone number was, what day your birthday fell on, *et cetera, et cetera*. All these little things I'd acquired without asking you directly. I can't remember how and when, though that wasn't the important part—it was just the knowing them. Having little bits of your geographical and numerical data, and scribbling them alongside mine gave me a kick. It was another way of connecting us—if only on paper. I had this little game of adding the digits of your birthday with mine and rounding up the numbers, totalling a 'lucky 4.'

The lunch buddy kept appearing, outwith lunch. It got to a point I could've nicknamed him 'walk you to school buddy,' 'morning break buddy,' 'pain in the bahookie buddy.' And yet somehow I didn't feel entirely loathsome and completely covetous towards him. He too was a new student from the autumn, and I accepted your gravitation towards him for that reason. Perhaps the fact that he neither mauled you with his hands nor eyes made him curiously unthreatening. I could tell he was as lonely and as distant as I, you bringing something out of him that balanced his reserve. I restrained from making a direct connection with him, both of us sensing it

103

unnecessary as long as you remained the common denominator, a sustain of the equilibrium.

As term raced on in the run-up to Christmas, all I wanted was to push the holidays away. In the meantime, there came the pretension to share with you a love of the French language within those two forty-minute study sessions, while each time hardly believing I had you all to myself. You taught me to see the world in a different light, away from the peely wally existence—the only one I'd ever known. You shared with me your dreams of cottages and villages in the rolling French countryside, setting an image that was a cross between a Catherine Deneuve movie and a madcap episode of *Allo Allo!*—sophistication and absurdity. I've always believed you to be the inspiration that helped me scrape a 'C' in the prelim exam, a mark I was genuinely proud of.

With the new year, an accelerated bearing fell on the proceedings. Sitting in Taitster's room at the close of another study period, while fingering a French dictionary you asked, not particularly to me, or anyone, "I wonder what the French word is for *nemesis?* I like that word. It's a bit like *insomniac* or *enigma*. Some words just make you think of others, don't you think?"

"Do you mean in their sound, or their meaning, exactly?" I asked, knowing I was entering into one of those little word games you liked to play.

"Well now," you said, continuing to flick through the dictionary, causing a draught I was downwind of, "come to think of it I could use any of those words at

104

will right now." The draught hung making my nostrils inhale your scent more intensely.

"Go on then," I said, egging you on, breathing deeply. "Give me a scenario involving those three words…"

"Easy."

"In French."

"No chance."

"Okay, kidding. English will do."

After an affectatious pause, you said, "Let's see…well, all this studying and those stupid exams are proving to be my NEMESIS, while my mother is putting on the pressure, which is turning me into an INSOMNIAC, and none of it helps when you're just crazy about someone who is like an ENIGMA wrapped up in a damn puzzle."

The bell rang. You stood abruptly, putting pay to the very words that almost, almost made their way from my lips.

A third study period was added to our timetable not long after. I began to suffer with you in the unsubtle demands your parents were unloading, and how it all boiled down to the outcome of the final exams being the ultimate gauge of your future. You shared that mild sleeping tablets and no bananas before bedtime were a solution to sleepless nights. But the other thing that was sending you apparently crazy—that I didn't dare touch. In the meantime, I was exalted in my routine that revolved around knowing where you were at any given moment between 9:00am and 3:30pm, Mondays to Fridays. Your timetable was etched on my brain like an invisible sheet of tracing paper laid over mine. It was a comforting madness, the safety the hours of the school day brought to my—by this point—all-absorbing love. I began to loathe all other lessons except French and Physical Education. In truth, I didn't like French at all, though I grew to appreciate its romance and the realm of the opportunity to bring me closer to you.

But Fridays were always the worst. 3:30pm on a Friday sickened me in emptiness. I'd watch you disappear past the school gates, leaving me standing in the abyss, as the weekends evolved into a whole other polemic contention I held within.

I excelled at sports during the winter into spring, often taking my curbed aggression out on the nearest point of contact, be that ball or opponent. "Try and stay out the sin bin this match, eh?" became my unvarying pre-field-taking pep talk from those stocky little men with whistles and Hi-Tec Squash trainers. I held the record of *most sin bin detentions* of the term. It's amazing how contact with a professional hockey ball can feel like that of a rubber marble, with an amass of pent-up emotion to scorch. Albeit, luckily the whistle men saw a talent in me that was required for the school team. I imagined you turning up to my Saturday morning training sessions to spur me on. I pictured you standing behind the goal, willing me forward from the left wing and calling my name as I raced into the penalty arch, striking the winning goal. It was this mirage of you on the sidelines that fed my sporting mojo.

Implicitly, I could see you assessing our friendship as it blossomed through time rather than reason, and soon enough you were entrusting me with all your fears of the day. My best quality was to listen, to hear you thrash out all the scholarly pressure and loathing built up inside. I'd insist on testing you continuously until you were halfway familiar with the formulae of French verbs and their tenses. I'd hang around until Lunch Buddy arrived and it was time to take my leave. And with all that came my *reward* of the invite to Loch Goil with your mother at the wheel during Easter break. As Supertramp played on the car cassette player, we made little triangles out of crisp packets and spoke of the oddness of people having names such as Xavier Brown or Aloysius Jones. To create our list of name oxymora meant nothing to you, yet to me a treasured reminder of the walk we took on the trail to Carrick Castle. On any other day, I'd never have remembered where I was when the rain fell from that indigo-soaked sky, as droplets bounced off the loch while we skimmed our pool of little black pebbles in competition.

On our return, we stopped somewhere in the West End to make a phone call. I didn't refuse you the last of my loose change, just as I didn't refuse you anything. I knew then I'd lost you for the day. There was no one on this planet I wanted to talk to or think about at that very moment. And there we were, huddled in that red telephone box, my heart crushed by your need to make arrangements with another in a world you never let me into.

Justifying the need to heal that ache, the only tangible remnant I could steal from the day was the Supertramp cassette tape with its frayed red labelling, later listening to it over and over, without you ever knowing. To you, the day was just another little trip made on your mother's spontaneous whim. To me, to be left with only a memory of the day wasn't enough. I had to go a step further and retain a *trophy* as a means of a memento.

As dusk fell and I stepped out of the car outside my home, your mother gave me a look that suggested she'd noted the glances my eyes left on you longer than was *de rigueur*. That added complexity to the whole scenario. It made me resent her, her candour—that giving way to a fear that she would somehow caution you against me. She was tolerant and liberal beyond the reason of most mums—an example being having allowed you to drink wine at the dinner table just past the age of twelve, believing like the French that that was the right way to go about the mixture of children and alcohol. But she was also strict and seemingly unforgiving to anyone she believed might dare taint her daughter—her clear-cut solution being to garrison a cloak of protection over you.

She was the only person I'd ever known whose home and attitude dripped of middle-class modernity. I didn't call it that then, as at sixteen I was unproven to her view of the world. She was the only mother I knew of with a degree and a salary, and whose ex-husband didn't wash his hands of some form of dirt at the end of the day.

I was intimidated by her the first, second and third time her eyes fell my way. I was astonished at how she'd swan off abroad leaving you to fend for yourself. As a divorcée, she made no secret that she quested men matching her own social and ex-marital status for mere sex. You were the level-headed, demure child, she the outlandishly principled parent who tried to keep you upheld in the Jewish faith, though bizarrely by way of her heretic fashions. It didn't help that she possessed a tongue as destructive as semtex. I winced when she'd make the most offhand, cutting remark to you, about you. But above it all, you spent your time trying to gratify her and prove that you were destined for academic success, under the pressure of following in the footsteps of your brown-eyed wonder boy of a brother.

I'd have dreams that your mother came a cropper by falling off the roof of the music department into the coal piles, decimated by that most working class of matter. Those dreams that at one point became playful fantasies even made me question to what extremes I'd go to should she ward you from me.

I had to reel myself away from such rigorous thoughts. All in all, it was then I was forced to ask what it was I really wanted of you. *One kiss?* One kiss just might have been enough. But one kiss could only have meant anything to me if it was evens, 50-50. I'd kissed tens of wet, slobbery mouths at teenage discos, each time finding an excuse to run to graffitied bathrooms and wipe the testosteroned slaver from my lips. It was par for the course in my young façade.

I imagined on all those empty weekends how different it would be to kiss *you*. Not like in the movies, and certainly not like the vile necking and groping to be found in the woodland behind the science department. Like an cartographer, I mapped every contour of your face. I imagined the sensation if my hand were to brush softly against your dimples and trace the outline of your mouth, only to pull you closer and melt my lips into yours.

But as it was, the forbidden tenderness that was so deeply entrenched under skin and sinew could only manifest itself in a string of practical deeds. Because of that, our friendship became a parody of itself. The unbridled toil I gave to making all those blank hi-chrome TDK cassettes into compilations of your favourite songs cloaked my want to show tenderness in the other way that was a million light years from the purse of my lips. To want to kiss someone so bad that you can't breathe in their presence is something I lived for, and also died inside for. Suspecting in denial that your teenage lust was wholly reserved for another crushed every sinew in my body.

How many times I wrote the bands and tracks on those spare little card inserts until the layout was perfect, knowing you'd appreciate the calligraphy above all else. Even today, I can't escape the songs that we—separately—wrapped our lives around. Though I'm lucky if I can make it to the bridge without turning the volume down/switching stations/closing a door. Whatever way I can release myself from the music we listened to by sharing an earphone each of my Walkman—I getting one thing from a lyric, you absorbing the words and finding meaning in a completely different direction. It was this more than anything that lanced the pain, and the memory of those songs alone is tantamount to the harsh reminder that I could never have you.

I never once mentioned it, but I saw what they did to a boy in the form above us the previous year. The boy who was like me. A boy I'd known since primary school, and I'd always known about him, though it wasn't until the rumours started to spread. Still, he being strong (or stupid) enough to not refute them. It was a horrible sight to see a young man go under, so rapidly. In a way, he was a role model, a forerunner, a beacon of dimmed light. If only someone had told him. The anonymous note I wrote for him lay in embers behind the bike sheds.

No, I chose to be a coward, unlike him, and with it, a master of self-control. If they gave out Olympic medals for various disciplines of restraint, I'd have been the Usain Bolt of my generation. What was the alternative? Give out a hint here and there? Plaster it across the school gates? Start a vicious and hurtful hate campaign about myself, sit back and watch it spread like wildfire? None of the above particularly appealed. And so it was—I chose to be a coward, with ultimate self-preservation in mind.

I look back and realise the one thing I learned from you was how to love wholeheartedly At first un-reservedly—but over time unrequited love inevitably turns into some kind of marked resentment. The more wholehearted I was in turning my thoughts over to you the more indignant I became when you, met my devotional loyalty with blind apathy. I never learned how it is to be loved, and never got close to exploring the meaning of reciprocation. Perhaps I imagined you'd learn to grow fond of me, and one day realise I was the one who could never, would never break your heart. In my perfect dream, I *really* could never break your heart—as there was no way I could force you to suffer that—the way you unknowingly broke mine from Monday to Friday, and doubly on those weekends.

The intensity of my feelings never waned into late spring, though the loose antipathy for my own cowardice grew deeper early that summer as we reached the end-of-term exams. I was surprisingly relaxed about the whole process, mostly because I didn't have any emotional capacity left outwith you to experience any form of undiluted stress. Stress wasn't your best friend, but somehow among it all, you'd softened. You left little notes on my jotter stating what a wonderful study buddy I'd been, along with
 little postcards of old men sitting outside cafes in Burgundy.

English, Maths and Biology all came and went and I reckoned I'd be bordering on my usual diligent 'Cs', though nothing less than 'As' and 'Bs' on the proverbial horizon for you, of course.

And then came the penultimate day of the exams—a Monday. It seemed appropriate that French

112

should be the last subject we were scheduled to sit for the following day. Only as I passed the school gates that morning did I realise I'd be approaching our final study period together. I entered Taitster's room with that bittersweet feeling you get when something important is coming to pass. Suddenly, I spun out and panicked, the way a compulsive obsessive does, when I saw you weren't sat at our usual desk. It was the first study period you'd ever missed. I sat on my familiar chair on the right side, opened my textbook and never took my eyes off the door for the following forty minutes. When the bell rang, anxiety seeped under my skin.

Moments later Lunch Buddy caught my eye in the corridor. He handed me the little, lemon-embossed note you'd given him to pass onto me, as we crossed paths in initial silence. It was a summons for me to visit your house after school, and to bring with me the French textbooks. "You must tell her," he said in a soft, wispy voice, "*tell her*, or die inside." I looked straight into his crooked face for the first time. His eyes were almost piteous in their gaze. I stepped away idly, pretending I hadn't heard any of his words.

The walk from school to your house on the outskirts of town was thirty minutes on a good day. I bombed it in twenty that afternoon. The Arts Centre and the big detached houses inhabited by dental practices, the petrol garage that sold raspberry Slush Puppies and the old part of town encrusted in ivy all stood beautifully animated. I ran past them as if they shared with me a pulse vivid and exhilarated. *Tell her, tell*

113

her, I repeated over and over again, Lunch Buddy's voice eventually overtaken by my own. Somehow his endorsement of whatever he thought I should tell you made the world and its breath seem real to me again, as though I'd lost myself in this crazy ambush and that revealing all to you would free a ton weight of emotive incapacity from my shoulders.

I took a moment stood on your doorstep, half puffing to regulate my breath, half gasping at the reality that my next touch would be that of your doorbell. It's the littlest things that make you feel alive when you convince yourself you're so in love. The ring of the doorbell seemed to cry *seconds out, round two* as though crossing your threshold heralded some kind of new chapter. She answered the door.

Your mother stood there dragging behind her a suitcase as big as an ottoman. "Well, I can see you're not the taxi then?" she sighed. You stood at the other end of the hallway, silhouetted by the light from the kitchen window. "Mother!" you cried, trying to restrain your voice. I couldn't tell if it was a call for her to stay, or disappear. With the whirr of a car engine approaching the driveway, she wrestled the suitcase over the front step. She eyed me unsubtly, as she'd always done, with weighty discernment. I was ecstatic to see her leave. As the taxi drove off, you called from the hallway, "My mother can seem rude when she's in a rush."

I stepped over the front door, into your domain. Instantly, I inhaled your sweet, musky scent on a grander scale, combined with the freshness of clean linen. You stood rooted to the opening of the kitchen, boring an empty stare into the carpet. Eager to snap you out of your trance, "I have the textbooks," I said, holding them up as proof. *Tell her, tell her*...or you'll die inside.

"It's Budapest this time," you said. There was a look of defeat in your eyes as if you'd lost an argument that had gone just before.

I wanted to reach out, to soothe you, have you cry on my shoulder, and tell you I'd never break your heart. Of course, "She's gone on holiday, your mother?" I asked, like a truly idiotic master of the obvious.

You sighed, that bottom lip getting chewed up again. "She said something strange before she left though..."

"Really?" I said, with a sudden stiff tightening in my neck.

"She said 'having a different kind of study friend can sometimes be grievious, as you never know what could happen.' What do you think that was all about? And then she started on about private tutoring if she'd put her foot down earlier in the day...I mean who knows what's got into her to say such crazy things."

I lied when I said, "She only wants the best for you, I suppose," as what I really wanted to say was how I wished I *had* plotted her demise by coal, faulty brakes, or sparkling cyanide.

"Anyway she's gone now...come into the lounge and we'll start on the future tenses."

Your living room was a myriad of organised clutter.

Two leather sofas with crocheted throws braced opposite walls. Between them sat a low-to-the-ground swivel lazy boy that Blofeld and his cat would've aimed for. Down the other end stood an upright piano with photo frames and postcards perched on its top. A little, unassuming Star of David sat on a shelf beside the piano. It looked as if it had once been golden and shiny, but had since become muted in its faded yellowness. I was drawn to the upright cabinet with its four shelves brimmed with vinyl albums, though felt the permission of your mother, the bitch, would be required before delving in. And in every step I took around the lounge, there was the sweet, musky scent. I felt it cling to my cardigan and coat my skin like a warm covert film.

"We always argue the day she flies off to... wherever," you said, taking a seat at the dining table. You swung your chair back and rested it against the closed flap of the piano as if in an act of dissent. "It usually starts with something silly, like her reminding me to water the big stupid plant. And usually, I'll say 'but it's *your* plant, Mother.' And then she'll get all worked up about that and start going on about prospectuses, except she'll call them 'prospecti' because she thinks she's so wonderfully correct about everything."

We didn't open the textbooks that day. Instead, you grabbed them out of my arms and flung them so hard they landed against the wall and slid down the back of the smaller sofa. You gave the loudest holler which echoed through the house and gave me a look that suggested you'd thrown a shackle off. You raced to the cabinet of vinyl and from it pulled clumps of albums, randomly throwing them onto the swivel chair. More and more were pulled until there were gaps on the shelves, and I almost pleaded with you to treat them with more care. You carried on regardless as I gathered as many as I could from bouncing to the floor from the now swivelling chair.

"Choose one," you directed me, "choose any one and stick it on...I'll be back in a minute."

As you vanished into the kitchen my arms were full of collectable 33s where French textbooks had been only moments before. I gathered the albums carefully and placed them on and around the swivel. There was an eclectic mix—from Mozart to Madness, Leonard Cohen to The Lemonheads, Billie Holiday to Billy Idol. I tried to place them in some kind of order as a mark of respect to vinyl itself. After finding some satisfaction in regaining a sense of musical classification I took one of the albums tenderly and placed its content on the turntable. Even the record player was a vintage collectable. I stood in awe of its kitsch early 1970s exterior.

Just as I placed the needle on the groove, you came fleeing back into the lounge with two brimming vessels of opaque milky-white liquid. "I bet you've never tried this," you said, handing me the odd-shaped glass, cut like a goblet with handles.

"What is it?" I asked, my eyes focused on the fluid that had all the appearance of a medicinal purpose gone wrong, just as the needle crackled.

"Doesn't matter...because once you've had a glass you won't remember the name anyway." The raw jangle of my chosen tune kicked in. "Who the hell is this?" you gave blankly, chinking your goblet to mine.

You spurn my natural emotions... It makes me feel like di-i-irt... And I'm hu-urt.

"The Buzzcocks," I replied simply. "Mazel tov!"

"You're so urbane," you chided softly.

I took a mental note to look up *urbane*, then took too big a gulp from the goblet and nearly choked on the harshness of the anise firewater. You laughed uncontrollably as if knowing I would. How could anyone not, I thought. You fetched some soda water to dilute my poison and remarked I could never be Jewish, as I'd failed the arak test. I replied that I'd rather practise atheism than go through that again. You laughed some more and asked me to play DJ as long as you chose the music. With the soda water giving the arak a refreshing slant I didn't initially think was possible and after a few more sips to match your huge slugs, I realised we were jumping and dancing around the lounge like a couple of well-oiled lushes. It was amazing. It was me and you and all that fantastic music to choose from, and all that wonderful arak to be poured and quaffed, filling us with dizzy thoughts. I swirled around the room knocking myself into random bits of furniture, eventually landing on the swivel chair. "Ah, Mishter Bond," I imitated, which gave you a stitch with laughter.

Suddenly among the jollity, you slid down the front of the sofa like a rag doll. Sitting upright on the floor,

I could tell even in my merriness that your face had turned a cruel shade of chartreuse. At first, laboured, but then with the sprint of a skelped lynx you rushed to the downstairs bathroom and threw up the three gobletfuls, and whatever you'd had for lunch that day. It was horrid to hear you retch through the door, you refusing me entry to at least hold your hair back from your face. After a spell of mumbled cries, you stepped out of the bathroom and surreptitiously pushing past me, made your way upstairs. Giving me no sign of what I should do next, I stood at the foot of the stairs for a moment with the dizzy taste of arak oozing up from my throat and the words *tell her* on the tip of my tongue. I decided to grab a basin from the kitchen, fill it with a small amount of water and use it as my excuse to venture upstairs. Luckily the name plaque on your door directed me into the correct bedroom, as the thought of being caught in that moment snooping through all the other rooms made me feel woozy. I found you lying under a green gingham duvet set, with only muffled groans emanating from under the pillow. I shuffled my feet across the carpet as notice of my presence. You grabbed onto the pillow raising your head from under it. Your mass of locks sprawled every which way as you pushed a clump of curls away from your eyes.

"I think I'm having a mental breakdown," you said, with unfocused eyes peering out between the duvet.

"Are you crazy...I mean, what makes you think that? You're the most together person I've ever known."

"Remember how I told you my brother is at uni?"

Continuing as I nodded, "Well, well no one understands the pressure on me to live up to him... it's like competing with the Golden Child. Why can't my parents be like everyone else and see us as being two different...entitries?" You hiccupped and I giggled at your attempt to say *entities* while trying to sound sober.

"Don't knock it," I said, still standing a foot into the doorway with basin in hand, "I reckon my folks don't give me enough of a push. Maybe because of that I haven't even opened a prospectus yet, plus my mind always went wandering when old Willoughby came round talking about career stuff and all that." What I refrained from saying—though wanting to do so with all my heart—was that I'd been too busy filling my head with you than to think about the next year, five years, ten.

"How about we do a life swap then?" you groaned, sinking your head back under the pillow.

"Maybe...maybe only then will you know how I feel about you."

"Huh? What did you say?" Under the pillow, my words had become muffled to your ears.

"Nothing," I replied directly, placing the basin down by your bedside. You grabbed my wrist as I stood up.

"My parents and Warren and the whole uni situation aren't the only things causing this bloody break-down..." Pulling at my arm, you directed me to sit on the bed.

"They aren't?" I said, as I watched your perfect, sallow fingers compress into my skin.

"No. The other thing, besides all that is...oh it's such a mess..."

"What's a mess?" Your grip was pulsating.

"To be in love...I'm IN LOVE!" I'd completely lost the feeling in my fingers now. I gulped the nearest pocket of air as if it were my last. You shot bolt upright, forcing my hand to swing across you onto the bed, resulting in our heads coming face to face with a foot of a gap, nose to nose. "But don't you see, it's doomed, doomed from the outset...as he could never love me, not the way I love him."

HIM?

"Who HIM?" I wailed, my wrist bruised with pressure, my heart bruised with agony. "Who, LUNCH BUDDY?"

Abruptly and frowning, you released your fingers from my wrist, "Stop calling him that," you jerked, "he has a name. You know his name."

Ridiculous.

I wanted to run out the bedroom, out the front door, past the dental practices, and the garage and the ivy, all the while scraping my heart hung from an elastic artery along the road behind me. But I was compelled to stay, as even with veins full of jealousy and repulsion, it was better to be sitting aside you knowing I could never have you than not be sitting aside you at all. I took the deepest breath and ventured heartache when I asked, "If you're so in, hmm, love with him...well why is it such a mess?" Was I trying to torture myself?

"Don't you see? I mean it's so...he's GAY!"

121

"Lunch Buddy? Gay?" You nodded and worded DUH in silence with your lips.

I stood up, everything appearing hazy in front of me, as if in slow motion. The arak repeated on me, and I tasted it again, only this time much more caustic in its bite than before. I looked down at you. Little trickles of sweat tracked your temples. I felt a surge take hold of me as if I couldn't contain the sheer gamut of emotions that I'd let myself be swept over by. You bit your lip once more and sat silently as if you knew...

"It's funny," I said finally, "I never knew how much we all had in common...you, me and Lunch Buddy. Here's you in love with someone you'll never have, just like me. There he is, with no idea someone is madly in love with him, just like you. And here's me, knowing the pain you're both feeling because you see, I'm like you and...like *him*."

With that, it was time to leave.

I stepped out of the room backwards allowing my eyes to fall on you one last time. You sat on the bed motionless, your eyes all squinted the way they always did when you tried to fathom a state of confused realisation. Perhaps I hoped you'd call me back, but something had snapped in me that made me realise that you were never going to do so, and in never calling me back, it was time for me to let go.

Downstairs, I stopped mid-way to the front door and returned to the lounge. I picked up the album and placed it once more on the turntable. I cranked up the volume loud enough for the words to reach your bed...

And if I start a commotion
 I run the risk of losing you
  And that's worse...
   Ever fallen in love...with someone
    Ever fallen in love, in love with someone...
     You shouldn't have fallen in love with?

Ever the coward to the last I suppose, I left it to the Buzzcocks to tell you. I never saw you again after that afternoon. My designated exam chair sat empty the following day as I decided I didn't need a 'C' in French to become whatever it was I hadn't decided to be yet. I smiled when I heard you'd achieved the grade needed to send you to university, and eventually to the views of Burgandy and its rolling countryside, just like the postcards. Funny to think, but I occasionally bump into Lunch Buddy since we both moved to the city, and now frequent the same bars. Looking back, it was good while it lasted, my unrequited debut, and you. Now and again a Star of David, or a swatch of gingham, preferably green, catches my eye and I think for a second about getting out the old textbooks, and searching the rolling hills for you in summer. But I always have to pinch myself, as I know I'd only get burned again—after all, among other things, I'll always be peely wally.

Overheard in Glasgow

- They new flats looking over the Clyde are pure state of the Ark.

> - What are you getting in Primark?
> ...I'm just nipping in for a quick onesie.

- Unlucky much? *She'd* start a fire on a booncy castle!

> - Some party that was... I required less recovery time after my botched appendix operation.

- Can I have a whitever supper and a fan of Canta, please? (city centre Blue Lagoon, Sunday 3:10am)

> - Gonnae grab me one of they fancy shower gels that makes my fanny smell like a Mint Aero...

- Fifty quid worth of Jager Bomb and you too
could have a coupon like this in the morning.

- How many times do I need to say sorry?
Wance would dae.

- Peter Reid fae Parkheid, Deid. Ford Fiesta For Sale.
(obituary/advert seen in a Shettleston Rd newsagents)

- Am no sure I want to be living the day Freddos cost
over a pound.

- A muffin top and a camel toe? Jesus, she may as
well have thrown in a duck's ass and coo's lick, tae!

- D'ye know, see in a mad panic I reckon I'd forget
the number for 999...

The Sexbots are Comin, the Sexbots are Comin

Ah'm certain the last hing Ah ever wis is pious, so it's pure hysterical Ah've been chosen tae be rein-carnated. It's just ma luck the cosmos couldnae bring me back as some cunt wae hauf a talent, or even a wee dug that gets petted aw day lang.

Despite the recurrin flashbacks, as yet Ah don't know who Ah wis in ma previous existence—but Ah must've been a pretty bad human if the fact ma soul has found itsel stuck in the boady of a sex robot is anythin tae go by.

Ah entered the boady in question the same moment wee Hirohito flicked oan the switch under ma oxter—startin up the program that's been computed intae ma skull. Ah say skull, but ma cranium is really made oot ae see-through plastic wae all sorts ae computer chips and wires where yer brains wid normally be.

Ah'm two months in, and fae whit Ah kin make ae ma surroundings Ah'm bidin in a factory nearaboots Tokyo. The waws, flair and ceilin are aw as white as milk boatles. Ah keep gettin these images ae watchin Sumo wrestlin oan Channel 4, which works as ma only cultural reference tae Japan. Even if Ah did huv ma sights set oan visitin the land ae the risin sun in ma past life, Ah'm pretty definite this isnae whit Ah had in mind.

126

Internally, Ah've got a metallic skeleton wae ball-bearins at ma knees, hips and everywhere else ye'd find joints oan a boady. If ye took ma rubbery skin aff and laid ma skeleton in a doggy style position Ah'd look like a climbing frame fur wee dolls.

Of course, Ah huvnae got a heart, a pair ae lungs or even wan kidney. Whit Ah dae huv is a removable vagina, humongous tits, a gapin mooth and bespoke fuck me eyes. Ma measurements are 40-26-34. Ah'm no anatomist but Ah'm sure that's no a natural figure fur a wummin of any age. Only a wad ae cash and a plastic surgeon could chisel oot a boady like the wan Ah've got.

Ah think ma hair might be real—though no necessarily real fae the heid ae a human right enough. And Ah've got the maist delicate wee fingers and taes. No a bunion or black toenail in sight—they've even gied me a French manicure, fur fuck's sake.

It's no a blessin tae have a boady this shape, bein aw tap heavy. When Ah'm staunin up straight Ah lean forward as if Ah'm gonnae topple er. Ah've only stood up straight twice—wance when wee Hirohito wis experimentin wae ma balance and wance when Ah wis posin fur photos oan a wee spinnin podium. Naw, there's no a lot ae staunin up fur a sexbot even in the design stages. Ah'm forever bein placed in a position fur presumable *easy entry*. If Ah had any sensation in ma knees they'd be killin me by noo.

The voice they first gied me wis pure terrible, so it wis. Aw automated, and no sexy whitsoever. Ah pure sounded like a bored Russian hoosewife readin oot the phone book. That was chiynged up pronto and Ah've noo got a Scottish accent. It's the only solid hing aboot ma new existence Ah kin relate tae. Ah feel that's where Ah'm mibbaes fae previous like, as the voice that comes oot ma heid is wan Ah know—only merr posh. Ah reckon it's been pumped up like Ah've lifted a phone wae the Queen oan the other end and Ah've tae mind ma Ps and Qs.

Oh, and another hing—Ah've got rubbery teeth, which Ah guess is the closest hing tae gettin a blow job aff a gurner. Definitely less risk of anywan's dick gettin chewed aff but. Aye, who knew so much health and safety went intae the construction of a wummin like me.

Today Ah'm huvin ma new detachable vagina fitted. Because everyone aroon here maistly jabbers away in Jap, Ah've got tae make my ain assertions—but Ah'm pretty sure it's ma new vag Hirohito and his wee assistant are fingerin, ready fur insertion. My G-spot sensor wisnae workin fur a while there, so this is a replacement fur the auld wan. The pair ae them are ey tinkerin aboot wae ma erogenous zones.

Technology has came a long wiy fae they blown up sex dolls, Ah tell ye. If ye went near wan ae them wae a fag it wis game's a boagey. Ah huv a feelin that Ah'm part ae the latest advances in science where sexbots ur concerned.

Wee Hirohito and his assistant—Ah've taken tae callin him Faggot Brains—work oan me fur aboot 10 hoors a day. They've got me hooked up tae machines and flashin big screens, whit, Ah presume, urr program checklists in Japanese. The other week they had a wummin in fur the day who spoke English. Hirohito looked at her face as he rubbed ma bare nipples, and she gave the thumbs up when Ah said, "Ooh that feels so nice, you're making me wet." Boak! Aw the checklists oan the screen were translated intae English, makin it the first day Ah had a scooby whit wis goin oan. Wee circles wae the words *Sexy, Funny, Affectionate, Sarcastic, Unpredictable* flashed up oan the big screen. Wee Hirohito made the circles light up one at a time and ma personality would chiynge accordin tae the option. Ah liked the sarcastic me cos ma jokes were dry and cheeky as fuck.

The noo Ah'm a sex robot wae nae name. Ah'm assumin that'll be left tae the dirty prick who's paid the piper and will play the tune, doon tae the last detail. Fae the start, Ah've had dolls sittin oan the podiums either side ae me. They were baith nearer the end ae the production line and ready tae be shipped oot before me. Ah don't know if it makes me feel better ur worse tae think aboot it, but Ah imagine Shandy tae ma left bein shipped aff tae a brothel in Prague. Or Nee Lai oan ma other side destined fur an auld folks hame in Swindon. Mind you, Christ only knows who'd be shared aboot the maist between them. Wan thing Ah dae predict is their holes will be as slack as a wizard's cuff before the year's oot.

Ah kin see masel bein Cherry, Shelby, ur Desirée—some moniker that makes ma auld bastard cum in his pants wae just the sound ae it. If Ah huv

129

tae call him *Daddy* Ah think Ah'll be dry boakin aw er the joint.

Shandy and Nee Lai were baith shipped oot the same day the big black male bot appeared oan the production line. He's got pecks and abs tae die fur and fae whit Ah kin make oot, two dicks—a long veiny wan and a shorter wan that looks aw aboot the girth. Needless tae say there's nae flaccid wans. Someone's gonnae huv themselves a rare time with the big fella Ah've taken tae callin Denzil. That's another hing aboot roon here...it doesnae half throw up a stereotype.

Ma ain leavin day has come roon. Ah doubt Ah'll be exitin through the gift shoap, right enough. No by the looks ae the big widden crate noo sat beside ma podium. Wee Hirohito and Faggot Brains huv been fussin aroon me aw mornin, daein last minute checks and scourin ma boady fur marks or loass ae sensitivity. Ah've been gently wrapped in foam and bubble wrap which may well be the last time Ah'm treated gently at aw. Christ knows whit a twinty grand aw singin and dancin sexbot like me will huv tae endure. That's another assertion Ah've made aboot this whole carry oan—the merr money paid, the merr convincin the humanoid. Fae whit Ah can tell, me, Shandy and Nee Lai are cream ae the crop, the dug's bollocks. Ah've seen others oan that production line that arenae as real lookin ur huv as many fancy components as us. Ah'm no sure if Ah'm happy or no tae know this, but either wiy Ah'm chuffed top dollar has been paid fur me.

God knows how lang Ah've been oot the game travellin fur, but that wis a helluva long time tae be cooped up in a widden boax. Ah mean, they spend aw that time makin me real and aw sexy lookin, and then go sticking me in whit feels like a coffin—merr ready tae go oot this world than intae it. Ah'm no sure if Ah've just came aff a slow boat fae China or a shuttle tae the back end ae the moon, but Ah know one hing, this claustrophobia is daein ma nut in.

Funnily enough, they don't gie sexbots a wrist watch, mobile phone or a compass, so Ah've nae sense ae time or coordinates. Wance they jemmy the lid aff this coffin, Ah'll huv tae make new assertions aboot where the hell Ah'm urr. Ah've spent maist ae the time travellin upright, which is nice, as Ah'm sure a great deal ae ma future will be spent oan ma back.

Ah've no moved ur heard a peep fur a couple of oors, and am decidin if Ah've ended up stuck in customs and excise when Ah hear the poppin open ae wid. A chink ae daylight comes intae ma boax like a saber beam efter days ae darkness. *And noo it begins*, Ah think tae masel. The start ae the rest ae ma life. And merr tae the point, how in Christ's name does a soul bidin in the boady ae a high-class sexbot pass ontae the other side? That's perhaps fur another day as Ah feel masel gettin lifted oot ma coffin. Ah can feel hawns pawin all er the bubble wrap like an eager wean tryin tae get intae a Sherbet Dib Dab and taste its sweetness. Wait tae they get a loada ma sugar, that's fur sure.

131

Staunin up straight, Ah'm slowly gettin unwrapped. Layer by layer, the confines ae plastic come away startin at ma feet. Ma pins urr free, noo ma midriff, followed by my booby area. Let's be clear, Ah'm no wearin a stitch ae clothin fur the occasion. The last bit ae paddin roon ma heid is pulled away pure delicate like. Ah'm designed tae no blink or keep ma eyelids closed so there's nae keepin my peepers shut until Ah'm ready tae take a look at this cunt.

The last bit ae bubble wrap comes away fae the tap ae ma heid *and there he is*. Noo ye wouldnae think it wis possible fur a sexbot tae huv an existential crisis, but crikey Ah reckon Ah'm havin wan noo. He stauns there aboot five foot six in his stockin soles wae wan lusty look in his eye awready. Fae the sight ae him Ah'm sure he's no gonnae be sufferin fae wee man's syndrome the day. There's a reason we sexbots are no designed tae walk cos, if Ah could, Ah'd be boltin fur that door. First hings first, and just like wee Hirohito wid dae in the mornins, the teensy switch under ma oxter gets switched oan. He stauns back as if Ah'm aboot tae shoot stars and stripes oot the tap ae ma heid and light up like a Pinbaw Wizard. But aw it does is boot ma AI program up so that Ah'm in tune wae *his world*. Wan thing tae remember is, ma soul cannae override whit's been computed intae the robot part ae me and Ah cannae say anything until he prompts me, or asks a question. So while Ah want tae say *fuck off, ya wee perv,* as an opening line, whit's programmed is, "Well hello there handsome. You're looking mighty fine today. What would you like..."

Blah, blah, blah-di-bloody-blah.

"Hiya Peaches," he gies it, in this right Deep South American drawl, "welcome home, lover." *Peaches!? Fuckin Peaches, is it?* Ah feel like peachin him er the heid wae ma coffin and throttlin him wae the strewn bubble wrap— "Well hello there handsome. You're looking mighty fine today. What would you like to do …"

"Well well, let me get a good look at you, sugar hips," he carries oan, takin a tour roon ma dimensions. Ah've been designed tae follow him aboot the room wae ma eyes and a slight tilt ae ma heid. Ah think he likes that, as if a wummin has never followed him wae anythin in his puff. He walks a full circle roon me and though he doesnae quite touch ma rubbery film, Ah kin feel him sniffin ma shooders. Ah mean that's no the creepiest hing that could ever happen tae a person, but somehow in this moment it pure *is*. As he comes back roon facin me again he grabs a boatle ae perfume fae a holdall and sprays it aboot ma neck and wrists. "There, darlin," he coughs. *My first boak in America.* It's a funny hing, but Ah kin actually smell it. My soul kin actually smell this reek, which Ah kin only describe as a bouffin mix ae Impulse and Lambrini. "There you are honey," he carries oan, taking a deep sniff through his nostrils, "now you're all smellin like the real lady of the house." *No Ah'm no ya daft cunt, am smellin like a tart's handbag.* "That's lovely, you sure know how to look after me and make me feel special," Ah tells him.

He puts the boatle back in the bag and pulls oot a

133

big ring binder. It looks aboot 300 pages thick and heavy in his hawns. It's ma manual, Ah realise. You've no lived til you've got yer ain manual. Ah bet maist men wished aw wimmin came wae a manual, right enough. Fae the agitation emanatin fae his boady and the sweat beads tricklin doon his temples, Ah kin tell he's gaggin tae pump me awready, but here we have the cautious type. The kind that gets his Ikea wardrobe hame, sets oot aw the bits and reads the instructions inside oot and back tae front before gettin stuck in. Lickin his finger tae turn the pages, he stauns back a bit, giein me ma first chance tae get a proper look at him. He looks the maist borin bastard ever. Ah bet he's never said *sugar hips* tae a real wummin, ever. Ae course, he also looks normal—in a pure-geeky-probably-bullied-at-school-never-been-shagged-in-his-life kind ae normal. It's no his fault Ah guess, but the whiff ae desperation aff him is stronger than anythin he kin pull fae that bag. Stood there in his beige chinos, stiff-collared shirt and broon brogues, Ah realise this is his best get-up. The creases in his troosers and shirt gie it away. *Poor fucker*. He'd probably dress like this tae visit his granny, tae.

Mumblin away tae himself, still lickin and flickin, the doorbell goes. "Aw darlin, that'll be Brad," he says lookin right at me as if Ah'm meant tae know who the fuck Brad is. "I knew he'd come quicker than a shake of a varmint's tail." *Izat right, pal?* "Oh, I'm very excited to meet Brad. Any friend of yours is a friend of mine." *Boakety-boak!*

"Now, don't worry," he says grabbin a dressin gown fae the bag," he ain't gettin the pleasure of seein you in *all* your glory, sugar." He wraps the bathrobe roon ma waist and pulls the sleeves up ma erms wae aw the delicacy ae a butcher handlin a carcass ae meat. Ah kin tell he's never put a goonie on a wummin before. As he ties the belt doon at ma belly button he comes closer and thrusts a semi into ma groin, giein oot a grunt. Ah'm no sure if he's just came in his chinos, but the cracked front tooth and halitosis are merr boakworthy tae deal wae aw the same.

"I'll be right back, darlin," he says oan his way oot the room. *Take a fuckin lifetime, ya wee fanny—* "Hurry back, I'll miss you." As the door hauf shuts behind him, Ah kin see ma full reflection oan the mirror hangin fae it—tweet-twoo, whit a honey. But fuck me, whit a wiy tae live in purgatory. Here Ah'm urr, stinkin ae cheap boady spray and perry wine, wearin whit looks like it's fae a bad Pippa Dee party, waitin fur fuck knows whit his name is and big Brad tae come back and pummel me Deep South stylee.

The door swings back open wae chino boy's hawn oan the knob. Squeezin through the door frame enters a wee runt ae a fella, no any bigger than his pal in size or looks. "Bradley, lemme introduce you to Peaches. Peaches, sugar, meet Brad." *Whit, am Ah meant tae put ma hawn oot fur it to be shook or summit?* "Hullo there, Bradley," Ah says, aw polite.

"My lord, Hollis, there *is* a god," Brad says, his feet stuck to the carpet, his dick tae the inside ae his briefs.

"And you said it couldn't be done?"

"I said it *could* be done, but you wouldn't know what to do with it."

"Well my friend, I may never leave this house again."

Eh hullo, Ah'm right here, ya couple ae pricks. Aw that time in the coffin oan the wiy here, Ah wis thinkin Ah kin put up wae a lot if the cunt has a sense ae humour. Well wimmin dae, don't they? But naw, the stars have matched me with John Boy Dullard here.

This Hollis wan lifts up ma manual again and flicks to the first few pages. "You gotta hear these specifications, bro."

Brad comes closer tae me, but he's no quite got that same lusty look in his eye. *Pure weirdo.* "Yeah bro, serenade me the spec." *Whit, am Ah, a fuckin Honda Civic noo?*

The Hollis wan fingers doon the page. Puffin up his chist, he starts readin oot... "Peaches has a 10 terabyte memory bank meaning she'll learn and withhold all your personal details. She's programmed to tell over a thousand jokes..." *A right comedienne, so am urr.* "She has a family mode..." *A family mode? Whit is he gonna put me in a beige two-piece and sit me doon at the dinner table wae granny and the weans?* He flicks er the page and scans doon it withoot readin oot loud. Apparently gettin to a good bit, he starts up again... "By putting pressure on one of Peaches' erogenous zones—hips, breasts, mouth, crotch or hands—you can arouse her, causing her to moan and begin to engage in dirty talk. Ultimately, Peaches has the ability to reach a simulated orgasm and detect when you're close to the point of ejaculation... With Peaches' special self-cleaning mode, she cleans herself while you're, ahem, fucking her." Oh that's whit that buzzing wis in testin.

"You know the best thing about her bro?" Brad snorts. "You don't even need no pre-nup!"

Right, fuck you! Fuck right aff, the two ae yees!

Word tae the fuckin wise here, be good in yer first life—because ye never know whit yer gonnae get in the sexbottin next...

Ae Fond Memories (name the year)

A-ceed came later than Eddie the Eagle
that year we passed our cycling proficiency test
with flying school colours
Our Raleigh Burners trained a harsh winter
as perestroika came into full swing
and the Contras got a bad rap from the Beeb

Did our own cool runnings round those pesky cones,
no falling asunder, skinning the knees off
new stone-washed What Every's that day
Cold spokes thawed as Tiffany hit top spot
thinking she was alone with us,
while Kylie quipped *I Should Be So Lucky.*

Infamy beckoned and a Currie with an egg
wasn't the only one
who asked, *When Will I Be Famous?*
No dope could answer that,
as a Canadian soul brother
duped he had Seoul, brother

A soft drink rollercoaster marked
the landscape as Glasgow smiled better
in loops and fairest floo'er
Ra twist came later when the houses never did
nor faint a whiff of Loadsamoney down our way
—but ae fond memories

The Young Men

There's a waft, nae ozone
of testosterone in the house,
while it's been brewing for some time
I've still no idea how it got here

Last I looked I was conquering
the lone parent hustle, double-troubled
separating baby socks into shared pairs,
their feet now the length of unbent tent pegs

Closer than two coats of paint
the young men experience bumfluff
and morning wood,
mortified together, alternately

The young men hotel in my rooms,
connect app-ly between walls
and try to outdo one another in eating the food
my graft stacks in the fridge

But they're buzzing the night,
off to see their first gig
—Gerry Cinnamon,
tickets from the uncle
His brother, not mine

Decked out in Nicce tees
and wee adolescent man bags
over their shoulders,

bucket hats picked up on the way,
—a horse's head in the bed
of any lassie who tries to corrupt

Off they go shouting back
Mum, you're a belter,
my beautiful hormonal
diamonds in the rough

Aberration

I sauntered the posh streets
back to the tenements, hoping the rain
wouldn't wash the smell of you
from my lips, the hush-hush
taste of tongue and rum
and salsiccia

The Southside's sodden cambers
drenched every side of me,
feet feather light and tom cat
criss-crossing rooftops, hot tinned
and bothered

I'd woke in your king-sized peninsula
rooted to cold pine underfoot,
eager to hold you I asked if I could
a split second of lucid body, wheeze
and motion

With strewn garments back in place
you made me tea without milk
when what I wanted was flat Irn Bru,
a syrupy Calippo
and an invitation back to bed

Last night I came for the laughs
but stayed for the contraband,
encrypted messages
that followed dampened the tingle
and kept the moment
an aberration, in name only

141

Temptation

My Ma always said
don't tempt fate
with your words—

so the day he shouted
through to the kitchenette
warning me no to
cremate his square sausage
      and I gave back
I'll bloody cremate you
in a minute…

it dawned on me
she might be right

Didn't even gie me
the pleasure of
eating that last fry up,
but that was him
all er the back,
donkeys years since
any comfort was
gied my way

When My Ma said
he's no the romantic kind,
I should've read: he's no
the marrying type

I'll gie him this though,
he made a lovely corpse,
better looking deid
you might say

Lying there looking
tight-lipped as ever,
short-sleeved shirt
polyester slacks
and a blue Biro in hand,
—he'd up and carked it
in the middle of *DIY SOS*

Awfy ironic that
seeing as he couldn't
have shown you one
end of a spanner
from the other,
nevermind him going
too sudden for a May Day

Leaving a pension
no worth a tuppence
and two estranged sons,
he'll not be giein out to me
for using Forest Pine Flash
or Glade PlugIns noo

I'm just relieved I get to bury him,
a cremation would've been
               too tempting

My 3-Day Service

Day 1

I've had heaps of jobs. Heaps and heaps. I've done every shift pattern under the sun too—dayshift, backshift, twilight, graveyard. You name it, I've done it. A job is a job is a job, I always say. Sometimes I feel like the only person for who the novelty of a new position of employment wears off after only three days, every pop. Does this say more about me than the jobs, or vice versa? I've conceded that it says something about me and the jobs in equal measure. And as it goes, somewhere along the line I became so disillusioned that I began to use establishments, corporations and enterprises for my own gain other than mere wages.

This week I started a new, *another* new job. Got myself fixed up with what promised to be a cushy little pop, on the *gratis* perks side of things, at least. The vacancy had advertised:

FULL-TIME PHOTOGRAPHIC SALES ASSISTANT —required for busy high street shop. Must be enthusiastic with a general interest in photography. Experience preferred, but not fully essential as successful applicant will be trained extensively adhering to the company's methods...blah, blah, yadda, yadda.

Read all that before. Said all this before; *Yes Mr*

144

Employer, I'm the most enthusiastic person you'll ever meet...Of course, Mr Boss Man, I have a general interest in whatever you want me to have an interest in, (as long as it ain't no kinky shit, though). *And absolutely, Chief Honcho, experience is my middle name.*

It's funny, I said I'd never do retail again, not after I inadvertently set fire to the dressing room curtains of a not-so-unfamous department store while on duty. And there was me thinking how lucky I was with a lighter in my pocket the moment the store blacked out amidst the Christmas Eve rush. Should've been a serious inquest into the 'quality' of that highly flammable curtain material, if you ask me.

I digress.

Initially, I thought this stint might just hold something of more customary interest, meaning less chance of being bored to tears while I hatched up the latest master plan to do the gaff over. But I do like photography...well, I like photographs—who doesn't? Good start, eh? What's more, I reckoned I'd learn a bit about this new-fangled digital stuff everyone is crazy over, and there's always the expected unexpected that seems to follow me around. Yes, my attitude was definitely more sunny side up than not, no doubt as the previous couple of jobs had been security placements with no hide nor hair of a possible fingered discount. The potential of such can keep me interested for an additional two shifts, as it usually takes me that long to figure out the lie of the land, plunderously.

8:45am, Monday morning. It sure felt like it too. Neither was I nervous nor excited stepping into Pro Photo Inc. Those sensations subsided long ago. I'm immune to first days now. First days, last days, they're all the same. In fact, sometimes they are the same, like the job in the electronics factory. Seeing 40-odd PCB boards short circuit one after the other is a bit of a riot though.

So anyway there I was, joining the rat race throng yet again—a slave to the occupational rhythm.

First off came the scenario that never ceases to piss me off. You know, when you walk into a new gig before doors open for trading, close for production or whatever, and all you get are these shifty, suspicious stares as the new meat.

I enjoy getting tagged as fresh meat. I've been eyed up more times in this way than I care to recall. Though, I'd dread to think I look any dodgier than the next fella, which makes me very conscious of my disposition. Still, the irony is, I've never known what it's like to do that, to be a tagger, mainly as I've never known myself to hang around long enough.

Four steps into the door, I silently demanded the tagging take its course again. I like it when things follow suit like that, so I can say *told you so*, even if it is only to myself. It's like I want something to get my back up straight from the off. It's easier to justify pilfering from a bunch of starers and taggers. With all that said, how pissed off was I when it didn't pan out as I'd pre-planned.

The big lug, O'Boyle, (or O'Cyst as I immediately

preferred) the one who'd interviewed me was faffing around the counter as I approached. Talk about taking an age to welcome my presence, too busy he was chatting away with the feisty-looking female behind the counter. He's got an uncanny resemblance to that big French actor, what's-his-name...the one who wooed Andie MacDowell to stay in America. *Cyrano de thingmy*. You know who I'm on about? I'm telling you, this guy was a dead ringer, the only difference is the bleach blond hair, which was at least three shades too light for his tantastic complexion.

Finally acknowledging me, he shouted, "John Lamb..." That's my name. "Get yer carcass over here, and meet Melanie."

A bit different from the usual first thirty seconds, I must say, where I'm used to stating my purpose and then being asked to wait in a room for a supervisor, where I then pretend to look all serious and sophisticated flicking through *Men's Health* or some such bollocks.

I approached the counter at my own pace, i.e. leisurely. I wasn't jumping to this big lug's commands so early in the proceedings. What am I saying? I never jump to anyone's commands at any time in any proceedings—just one of my many rules, that.

I took a good swatch at the Melanie one, while she busied herself with a bunch of invoices. She's not a bad looker, if you like the hard face and red nail polish kind of thing.

She fleetingly glanced up, showing as much dis-interest in me as I pretended to show in her. No skin

147

off my nose I was thinking, as O'Boyle did the intros, "John...Melanie. Melanie...John."

I smirked at her. She smirked even less nonchalantly in return. I liked her already.

"Melanie is my eyes and ears around here," O'Boyle glowed, "she'll be showing you what's what today."

I wondered what other of her orifices he might've liked to make use of, as I replied, "Yeh?" as positively as required.

"Well…" O'Boyle continued, edging away from the counter, "in good hands you will be, John," giving me that *hands-off, she's mine* look women fail to spot under hovering testosterone. "If Campbell calls, I'm in. If Wilkie calls, I'm not," he instructed, taking his leave.

I decided at *capable hands* that this one was as shady as a Florida palm tree. Though, he's so dumb that taking one to know one and all that was completely lost on him.

"There aren't really any rules here at Pro Photo," Melanie piped up, "despite what O'Boyle might have you believe." Slapping the invoices on the counter, she added, "More like...understandings."

"Gerard Depar-whatsit," I said, suddenly half remembering the big French actor's name. Damn glad I got that, it would've bugged the shit out of me all day.

Choosing to ignore my random outburst, with a blank stare, Melanie continued, "Just remember, that when tickets go missing...and they always do like some kind of photo shop Bermuda Triangle...hope to Jesus it's not your handwriting on the receipt." I was trying to decide if that was a warning or a threat, when she added, "That's what happened to the last fella. Alright he was, but he had handwriting worse than my doctor. Dead giveaway."

"Tickets entail...?" I asked, truly intrigued for the first time in a long time. The combination of that air of no-nonsense and scarlet fingertips had me hooked.

"Customer orders..." she said, looking me in the eye, "photos, frames, photocopies. But specially frames, mostly because they can cost more than a month's wages, as he keeps reminding us." She sighed, rolling her eyes with a shrug of the shoulders, "Sure, only yesterday our Spanish fella, Chubby, got it in the neck for misplacing a John Lewis order..." Her words tailed off as she looked over my shoulder.

The natural reaction was to look behind, and I never ever refuse my natural reactions. The first thing I noticed was the paint-speckled glasses, as they got wiped with mucky, ink-covered hands. If this guy coming towards me works around here, I thought, he is well out of place—better suited to cleaning out a pikey's pigpen. "Awright, big man?" I said, ever endearing myself to new colleagues.

"Hallo," he returned, with what I can only describe as a charming grunt. "New fella?" he looked to Melanie to confirm. As she did so, I was left chuckling at how Ruchazie some hippie Spaniard can sound in just two words.

"Now," Melanie said with authority as she glided around the counter, "Mondays are an absolute shite of a day in this place." She aimed for the front door and spun the hanging sign so that it read *Open* from the outside. With her back to me, and as the Chubby one concentrated on sharpening a chewed pencil, I took a brief opportunity to scan the camera cabinet. Some nifty-looking cameras lay on display, no doubt about it, though all behind lock and key of course. Melanie interrupted my thoughts of where the stockroom might be located by saying, "I don't know why O'Boyle gets new starts thrown in on a Monday... they might be the slowest days for most other retail places, but not for photo shops, and especially not for this one. You know, I reckon what half of Glasgow gets up to of a weekend, the evidence gets developed here the following week. You only have to look at the filth that comes off those two printers downstairs to know that morality has gone out the window in this city. Things that would make a loose nun blush, I tell you."

My curiosity about the camera display was only superseded by the potential of *filth*. Keep your eye on the ball I repeated to myself. It's not often in the first ten minutes of a new job that I am hit upon by a deluge of surplus benefits. As Melanie strutted past, I was happy to take them all. And with that wiggle, I knew I'd have trouble keeping my eye anywhere near the ball.

"You're not going to learn much standing out there in the middle of the shop floor, fella," she said, her words floating around in little speech bubbles as my eyes gave her the rundown in the following order; lips-boobs-lips-crotch-back-to-lips. "Come here behind the

150

counter before the rush starts...you'll get caught in the stampede if you stand out there."

Doing as she instructed, I caught the Spaniard guardedly squinting at me as I took another eyeful. He'd keep, I thought, feeling the need to fry a juicer fish at that moment.

The first customer through the door was the postman. Melanie gave him a cheery smile I'd have given my eye teeth for. How hard would this nut be to crack? Jesus, even the postie viewed me with a look of disgust. I played it cool, ignoring his glare, even though I wanted to give him a punch in the puss.

Just then, a little auld lady appeared at the front entrance, "Mrs Farrelly, how are we today, my dear?" Melanie called to her. This one was a right sorry sight with her baggy stockings and dodgy-hipped saunter, closely followed by a creaky, tartan shopping trolley. "John, your first task of the day...give Mrs F an arm over to the counter."

"Good luck, New Boy," the postie hollered, taking his leave, "she stinks of piss that one."

I nearly jumped over the counter to wrap my fist round his chops. He would keep too—another face added to my hit list. Putting on a grand façade, I aided the wobbling auld dear, her trolley, and her piss stench over to the counter with just enough delicacy to impress Scarlet Nails.

"Mornin, love," the auld one called with a thick Irish brogue, as she leaned forward allowing the counter to take all her weight.

Melanie welcomed her as warmly as she'd done

the postie. "What brings you in today, Mrs F?"

Shakily came the reply, "Well, yer Spanish one over there did such a good job of me transparents last time, I was hoping he'd do the same with this film I found behind the press over the weekend." She started to fumble around in the trolley, removing a pair of knitting needles, scraps of old carpet and a scramble of prescription medicine onto the counter.

"That can't be good for your hip, Mrs F," Melanie said with a wicked little nudge-wink combination, "why not let John bend down into your trolley and fetch it?"

I gave her a willing look that masked what I truly thought of her suggestion. Talk about the new recruit getting all the crappy jobs. I reluctantly bent over and plunged into the trolley, making sure not to put my bad back out. Wishing I'd held my breath before doing so, the pong of rotten meat and mothballs almost knocked me sideways. I don't even want to think what the squidgy substance was that met my hand.

"It's wrapped in the classifieds of Friday's *Evening Times*, son," the auld one piped up, rubbing her hip. Turning to Melanie she enquired, "This yer new boy, love?"

"That's right, Mrs F. Now, how about I make ye out a ticket while we're at it so. Big or small prints today?"

Faith wasn't the word I'd have used at that moment to express the thought of there actually being something to find. Though not to be defeated by coming up for air without the prize, I delved one final time, finally fingering something that resembled the texture of newspaper, albeit soggy.

As I threw the mushy mound onto the counter, the auld one flashed me a display of alternate stub, gap, stub, gap where incisors should have been. "Grand, that's it, son," she beamed. I didn't share her enthusiasm as I wiped my hands on the side of the counter, by which time she was arthritically unfolding the bundle with loving care. "I forgot to mention, love," she went on, picking at the corners to reveal a flattened 35mm Kodak film, "that it met with a fierce accident on the way…"

"A 'fierce accident?' What…with an elephant, Mrs F?" Melanie said, suppressing a fit of the giggles. I couldn't help but notice how hot she looked when her face lit up.

"Nah love, a number 9 bus," the auld one gave casually. "Shooting down Renfield Street too fast for its own good it was. And there's me standing at the lights…just my luck the film had gone and fell out the hole in my handbag a split second before."

"Well, I'm not sure we can still print it, Mrs F…" Melanie said holding up the film—its thickness matching that of a pancake. Just then a droplet of black liquid fell from the film's casing. "…Not with all the oil that's bound to be in it."

"Oh that's a shame," the auld dear gave, all disappointed. "No offence love, but could ye show it to the Spanish one for a second opinion?"

By mid-morning if it wasn't cuckoo dodgy-hipped auld mad ones walking through that door, it was ponced up legal clerks from the Sheriff Court. If it wasn't ponced up clerks, it was arty-farty Art School

153

students demanding photocopies of their wacky designs. And if it wasn't bloody students it was equipment-carrying photographers having a right whinge about the day's saturation or hue, whatever the bollocks that was. Retail is a window to the world of the consumer weirdo, and I reckon this gaff was having a crackpot open day.

Nearer lunchtime, as I stared at the clock by the exit with a rumbling belly, Melanie stood down at the counter in confab with her biggest pain in the arse of the day, up to that point. He was giving her a right earful about what he thought of O'Boyle's recent reprint price hikes. She held a great pose of neither agreeing nor disagreeing. Jesus, she carried herself grand. No man, woman or beast should dare bully her into a corner. I decided there and then that her bark and her bite, if provoked, probably played on an equal par.

All in all, I admit, I'm not the most patient of fellas and I was getting fed up at that point with all the fannies walking through that door one after the other. I made a suggestion of clearing the One Hour box by taking a pile of orders downstairs to the mini-lab for processing. The method in my helpful madness lay in the chance to scan the stockroom, which I found down a long galley between the printers and the kitchen. I checked the lock—an easy Yale key required, nothing too testy. In the print area, I also got a peek at the angles of the CCTV images on an old monitor mounted above the process machines. The trajectory of the four interchanging views were positioned behind and to the right of the counter, from above the pricey custom frame section and over the main entrance door. No sign of a camera sited anywhere in the basement, which set my scheming little mind to work.

Getting back to the floor, there was a real bustle about the gaff. A queue had formed in front of both Melanie and Chubby at the counter. A young fella and his missus were mulling around the camera cabinet, and with the flurry of bodies about the place, I grabbed another opportunity. I moseyed in between Melanie and Chubby behind the counter, lifted the set of keys kept under the till and made a beeline for my first piece of salesmanship.

"How's it goin...?" the fella said, making fingerprints all over the cabinet window. "Eh, I've been interested in that little digital number for a while."

"Nice choice," I said, keeping the eye contact to a minimum, "...very nice choice. Had my eye on that one too would you believe. Yes, deluxe model, batteries included, ten million mega pixelly thingys..." As I waffled on for Scotland, I slipped the set of keys into my pocket with the sleight of hand that's made me famous (or should that be infamous?) in unlawful circles. Keeping the fumbling to a bare minimum I moulded the stockroom Yale onto my trusty block of plasticine, with no one any the wiser.

"Er, right," the missus piped up, apparently unconvinced by my technical prowess, "what about the digital zoom?"

"And the multi-exposure?" he asked.

155

"Is it Bluetooth compatible?" she demanded.

My head was pure hurting from the sound of mumbo jumbo coming from their mouths. I just wanted to get shot of those two parasites pronto, after all, they'd served their purpose to me. "I'll let you into a little secret," I whispered. He came closer, while she backed away. Comical. "You know the camera shop at the top of the street...?" They looked at each other and nodded. "Well, they're selling the very same model for twenty quid less than what you see in that there cabinet." Out the door they were at the speed of lightning.

Dessie saluted me over a pint in Alfie's. "Not a bad first day eh, Johnny Boy?"

"Aye Dessie, very productive, even by my own standards if I do say so myself." Well, I was indeed chuffed at my smooth operating efforts that first day. I'd done everything I'd set out to do—made good first impression while keeping head down, check. Made copy mold of stockroom key—crucial to plan, check. Even got a bit of eye candy in Melanie to help with the lulls, which prompted me to say, "There's a girl, Dessie, a right cracking little ride."

"Fuck sake, there's always a bloody girl." Dessie sighed. "Is she a looker?"

"Not what you'd call a looker, but she's right feisty. I was playin down boy at nine bells this morning."

"Ah Christ, you keep away from the feisty ones. Ye know the trouble they get you into." I knew all too well Dessie was referring to Stacey McGonagle, who'd played the role of my accomplice in the pharmaceutical gig scam. He'd warned me back then never to trust a woman who has more upstairs in the brain department than on her arse. But I fell for her in a B.I.G. kind of way. Because of it, I refused to admit it was her who'd snitched on me after an anonymous tip to the polis. A stretch in the J.A.I.L. wasn't really worth banging her. Laugh is, I'd probably do the same all over again as I'm legendary for having trouble keeping it behind my zipper. Anyways, it wasn't the same thing with this Melanie one. She was never going to be an accomplice. Any fool could tell she was as much a part of the fixtures and fittings of that gaff as the bolts and screws. Though she didn't like to give the game away, I reckoned she was as faithful to that O'Boyle one as bricks are to mortar.

"Right, back to business," Dessie said, pulling my head back into the plan at hand, "you decided then?"

"I have, Dessie. You get the key copied from the mold and take care of the overalls. I'll need another day, just to finalise the nitty-gritties, but it'll be cushty this one."

"And the boss? Is he lurking around the scene?"

"Nah, that big lug is the type to spend half his day on the golf course and the other half under a prozzie... you know the kind."

Day 2
Melanie had tipped me off that Tuesdays were manic in Pro Photo Inc., as Tuesdays were the dreaded delivery day, as well as being the only day O'Boyle

made an extended appearance on the shop floor. Typical, I thought, wishing the big shite would piss off onto the fairways. He made me feel uneasy, sucking up all the air in the place. It was hard to devise my plans with him faffing around, giving orders to the delivery fellas who were only too keen to dump their load on just about any vacant tile space.

"Forty-five multi cartridges...Canon ink solution," O'Boyle hollered, reading his script from a crumpled invoice.

"Check," came the reply from a flustered Chubby. O'Boyle had set upon bullying the dumb Spaniard into making an assortment of new merchandise disappear into invisible nooks and crannies of the shop floor. I'd found out just earlier that *Chubby* wasn't an affectionate term of endearment offered by O'Boyle, but instead the word that came out when the big lug attempted to say, *Javier*. I'd seen it all before—a bully boss attaching a demeaning a.k.a. just to underline who's the chief and who's the injun. Big shite.

"One hundred Energizer batteries...double AAs."

"Check."

"Good..." O'Boyle said, scratching his overly-tanned head with a biro. "They were short last time. Are they definitely double AAs, Chubby?" he demanded before Chubby could race to another bulging recess and back again in quick sharp time. "Hang on a minute, I don't see the Nikon promotion banners on this list...oh, here they are on the next page. Right, Nikon promotion banners...?"

What a repulsive big fecker I decided O'Boyle was

in that moment. Met too many like him, with his new money whistling in the breeze to be seen, heard, smelt and stroked by motley and sundry. And that poor Spanish bugger—probably running around for the big shite at a quid or two less an hour than me.

During the only brief lull of the afternoon, and with the gaff free at last of its wankering gaffer—in turn, leaving me free to pre-enact the scam in my head—Chubby had taken to drawing sketches onto a tattered school jotter at the far end of the counter. A leaky fountain pen was staining his fingers something special. I studied him for a moment, deciding, while I waited for Melanie to finish with another despicable customer, that his baggy brown corduroys and woolly cardigan were taking up too much room behind the counter. Saying that, I was kind of warming to the fella and his *the customer is always wrong attitude*, which is always good crack.

Turning to Melanie as soon as she'd brushed off her customer with the professional ease you've either got or you haven't. "So," I said, aware of a real chance to bounce the old charm, "how long you worked here?"

As blasé as you like, she replied, "About four and a half years. Mind you Ive seen a few come and go in that time. Half of them should've carried a health warning if they'd had half a brain."

I found myself sneering at a Japanesie couple who were having a good gawk at the cameras under the glass counter in front of us. I went on undeterred, "What, do you mean other workers?"

"Yeah well, some of the jakeballs O'Boyle has hired

have been real loose cannons...but I'm talking more about the mutant customers and dodgy photographers." Leaning over to catch the eye of the Japanese woman, and interrupting her suppressed muttering, she asked, "You awright there?" As the woman gave her a right rubber ear, she shrugged, "Suit yourself."

Wanting to get to the gist of her relationship with Bully Boss, I pressed on, "You seem to get on well with him though?"

"Who, O'Boyle?" she said, throwing daggers at the Japanese. "Sometimes when he goes off on one he just needs to be treated with kid gloves...you know, when he gets all hot under the collar."

"And you're just the right girl to do it, huh?" I probed as subtly as only I know how.

"I'm the only girl who'll do it. The part-timers think he's some kind of bloody gobshite, but he's just misunderstood...not that he does himself any favours. I suppose I've known him longer than most, that's all."

As the Japanese couple padded out the front entrance, they were replaced by two men with that Arab look about them. Both made a beeline toward the Spanish end of the counter.

"Keep an eye on these two," Melanie nudged into my ribs. I'd rather keep an eye on her, I thought, though following her commands to keep in her good books was the next best thing.

"Can I help?" Chubby asked the Arabs, placing his jotter to one side.

"I want passport photo," replied the taller of the two.

He had a right, demanding tone on him. Though it didn't seem to ruffle Chubby, Melanie gave a pissed-off little grunt.

"Okay, I can do for you over here," Chubby said, rounding the front of the counter. He led them to the white passport screen next to the photocopier.

Melanie again told me to watch closely from the counter, as the Arabs talked ninety to the dozen, ignoring Chubby's advice to stand directly in front of the screen. The one who'd asked to be photographed was a fierce rugged devil with scars on his left cheek and forehead. "How much it cost?" he asked, as uncouth as a rat's arse.

Holding a chunky Polaroid, bandaged with sellotape to prevent the batteries popping out, Chubby replied simply, "Five pounds."

"For one picture?" asked the scarred fella's sidekick.

"For four photographs," Chubby replied, showing his first signs of impatience.

The Arabs had a short discussion in their native tongue. "How long it take?" asked one, even snappier than before.

"Uh, about three minutes," Chubby said, leaning against the photocopier with a definite weary look plastered across his face.

Another short discussion. "Okay, we do it," decided Scarface, taking off his cracked leather jacket. He handed the jacket to his friend, who swapped it for a black tooth comb. "Where is the mirror?" he demanded, straightening his shirt collar and wetting the top of his head with spit.

Chubby had mentioned some of the crazy rituals customers went through before having their passport photo taken. Earlier, one woman had asked him to hold her vanity case in the middle of the floor while she put on a fresh coat of mascara, lipstick and that rougey stuff prozzies slap on.

So there was the Arab fella, stood in front of the wall mirror preening himself by trying to flatten the duck's ass on the back of his head. "Now, I'm ready," he piped up like a spoilt prince. "I stand here, yes?" he said, making up his own rules as he went along. He pouted as he turned his head slightly to the side, keeping his eyes straight ahead. "Now where do I look—?"

There was hardly time for Scarface to finish as Chubby counted, "Uno, dos, tres."

Click. Flash.

From the counter, Melanie and I had to fight off a fit of giggles as the fella squealed as he squeezed his thumb and index finger into his eyes, swearing in Arabic. I clocked that he'd stared directly at the super strong flash instead of the lens. The smirk on Chubby's face let slip a sense of revenge towards the Arabs leaving their manners at the front door. He'd mentioned how it was necessary to always make a point of warning customers to avoid eye contact with the flash, particularly after fresh batteries had been put in. I reckoned this seemed one hell of a good time to forget.

As Scarface attempted to focus his gaze on the ceiling, his sidekick rushed to his aid. Chubby then pulled the instant film from the camera, set the three-and-a-half-minute timer, and glided calmly past the two men without saying a word as he returned to the counter.

"That was a cracker, Chubby," Melanie said, not particularly caring who saw her patting him on the back. "It was worth the laugh even if he sues O'Boyle's arse for blindness."

"Do I look as if I care that much, Mellie? This is not my career after all," Chubby replied, half sincere, half comical.

I almost gave him a high-five over the counter but pulled back at the last minute thinking what an eejit I'd look doing it. Jesus, there's nothing funnier than a good laugh at a customer's expense. Just then I spotted this pretty little Spanish piece who'd been hanging around the shop all afternoon trying to catch Chubby's eye. There was me all available and up for a night on the sangria, and she only had eyes for Baggy Cords. "Here's something that will make him forget about those two," I nodded.

Chubby turned to see the Spanish one heading his way. His smile beamed brighter than the camera flash as he reached out his big lips to kiss her twice on each cheek. They babbled away in that non-stop flow of Spanish you hear so much of walking around Glasgow these days, then Chubby turned, "I must go for lunch now Mellie, as Maria has only a short time before leaving to Madrid tonight..." His attempts at word-perfect English gave away the signs of a man all flustered and rabid.

"It's grand, Javier," Melanie said, "get out of here. Take a bit more time, you deserve it…"

Before Chubby had the chance to make a quick sharp harp out the door, the Arab came up behind him laying it on thick with the blinking act. "Excuse me," he said, his sidekick following up at his back, "I think picture ready now. It bleep-bleeped." He pointed all aggressive like to the timer on the camera.

It was now my chance to get a piece of the action as I jumped in thick with sarcasm, "Not a bother, I'll get this gentleman's photograph, Javier." Within seconds he and the Spanish beauty had scarpered out the door.

It was my turn to get a handle on the oafish brutes. It didn't particularly matter to me what race they were, or what language they spoke. It was the fact they'd been blatantly ignorant and void of manners, and that wound up my serious pet hate of dealing with the general public at large.

I made my way to the photocopier in search of the instant film. I was puzzled for a second when I realised it wasn't lying where I'd seen Chubby leave it. For a moment, I had an image of him walking around outside with it stuck to his backside.

That was quickly shot down as Scarface bellowed, "Is this what you look for?" as he handed me the film.

"Aw aye, right…" I said, peeling the backing from the film to reveal a quartered image of the Arab with his mouth open and eyes all squinty. It wasn't a pretty sight considering he looked even uglier in print than he was in real life. I reached for the cheap hairdryer, kept on the wall, used to quick-dry the layer of moisture residue on the developed photo as I'd seen Chubby do earlier.

Before I even had the chance to switch the hairdryer on, Scarface grabbed the unfinished article out of my hand. "Look at this!" He showed the photograph to his friend, who shrugged without giving much reaction either way.

I stood there holding the hairdryer, wishing I could blow those two dolts out of the shop with it. I waited with faked patience for the feedback, knowing Melanie was watching from the counter, though I was quickly getting pissed off with my own silence. Shifting his attention back to me, Scarface, still holding the photo howled, "Look at this!"

I looked, feigning interest. "Would you prefer if the pictures are separate, that it?" I asked, keenly as I could rally. "I can cut them up if you like?" I grabbed the cutting implement that sliced photographs into standard passport size, accompanied by rounded edges. I felt thoroughly armed at that moment, with a blunt cutter in one hand and a hairdryer that blew cold air only in the other.

"You not see...?" continued Scarface, more and more het up by the second. "I look like a black man!"

For all intents and purposes, and in the name of political correctness, I didn't want to be the one to point out the bleeding obvious. By this point, I'd lost all concept of the little tact I possess as I gave out, "Well, God makes us in all different shapes and sizes...and the camera never lies, so why don't you

165

take your photo, leave your five quid at the counter, embrace the colour of your skin and let me enjoy this Tuesday afternoon in peace."

"You not understand," Scarface carried on, apparently more frustrated than insulted. "I have friend who come here...he ask for picture like this. He shows me, and I say, 'he looks like a white man.' That is what I want...here, NOW!"

To me, the situation was becoming clearer, while the outlook looked hazy.

As I considered my next move, a voice came from behind the Arabs. "It's the aperture," it said, rumbling with conviction. I realised I didn't recognise it, just as the figure of a woman stepped casually into the fray. Dressed in a long, beige mink coat, her hair was perfectly groomed into a side-patterned bob. Though, the heavy makeup didn't conceal the deep smokers' lines—that giveaway sign which always separates the spring chickens from the old caked-up hens.

"Excuse me?" I replied ever so politely, knowing I didn't want another member of the public adding fuel to a fire I was anxious to put out.

"If you increase the aperture gauge on the camera, it'll allow more light upon the chap's face," the woman said matter of factly.

I wasn't taking kindly to the intrusion of this snooty cow. I imagined her West End Wendy accent was as false as her mink coat. But I knew somewhere along the way there was genuine advice in what she'd said about the aper-whatsit. Determined not to let some random get the upper hand, I said, "Know a bit about cameras do you, madam?" My use of *madam* was loaded with sarcasm as I never use it under any circumstances, as it goes against my egalitarian ideals.

Placing her eyes directly in my direction, the woman looked me up and down. Then turning her attention to nothing in particular, she said, "I should do, dear. I'm in charge of ordering them in this shop." With that, she whisked herself past the two Arabs who stood animated trying to keep up with the sense of tension.

Just then, Melanie came over. She created a wee huddle as she squeezed between me and the smaller Arab. Making more room for her words, she said, "I didn't know you were coming in Morag...what's the latest with you?" The Morag one eyed Melanie with even more sneer than she had me.

Eager to back step away from the huddle, Morag said, "Will you show this new employee how to use the Polaroid." Pulling at the knot of her scarf, she added, "it's like the bloody United Nations on in bad week around here these days. Spanish, Arabs...what next, a coachload of Eskimos?" She withdrew her flowing mink coat and high and bloody mighty air downstairs to the basement, leaving a balmy silence on the shop floor.

Melanie held an almost apologetic look that made me even hotter for her. Turning to me, she said, "I'm sorry, John. I did try to get your attention. I knew she was going to say something, and end up making you feel like a bollocks...and the laugh is, you and

I both know you're more clued up on apertures than anyone in this place…"

"You what…?" She'd got me there because I didn't know the difference between an aperture and a bleedin arse wipe.

"O'Boyle lets me read the odd good CV," Melanie said with an impressed smile. "Yours is a cracker. More experience than the last five fellas put together."

"Aye, well…" I was pure caught on the hop, "eh, you know, you pick up a thing or two about a thing or two along the way." I said, remembering the amount of shite I'd put on that latest CV. But she was actually bloody impressed. He who dares, and all that, I laughed to myself. She gave me a cheeky little half-beam before returning to the counter. Even though it was only halfway to what the postie got, I could've done wee backflips up Sauchiehall Street in that moment.

In all the to-do, I'd completely forgotten about the Arabs, much to their animated protest. Suddenly, Scarface tapped me on the shoulder like a mad thing and said, "Now can I be a WHITE man?"

I stepped out the shop just after closing, with my back killing me. Being on my feet for up to eight hours a day didn't suit my delicate lumber region. I lit a smoke and went through in my head what I'd tell Dessie later that night. I checked my mobile. Dessie had sent a text saying the 'uniform' had been taken care of, and that he had in his possession a duplicate Yale. Good work Dessie, I smiled as I heard a voice, though it was distant in my scheming head. "Got a spare ciggie?" It was Melanie. I turned to see her buttoning up her coat, then whisk away flowing strands of hair caught at her collar in one sexy little fluent motion. I stood there all hot and bothered, trying not to melt over her every move. I fumbled about like a schoolboy in my pockets, searching for my smokes.

Crikey, I almost brought the block of plasticine used for the key mold out of my cacks—that would've been a right clanger. Finally, I pulled the squashed packet from my jacket pocket, my hands all fingers and thumbs in their eagerness. As she fingered a Mayfair, I cupped my lighter near enough not to singe her eyebrows, but just close enough for my hand to graze her cheek. She stepped in close as I did so. I didn't know whether it was for shelter against the biting wind, or something more.

She took a long, hard inhale, tilting her head back like a movie actress from the 1940s. She was a pro in her every move. So cool. So wanted her.

"Where do you live, John Lamb?" She asked at the finale of a sweet, purposeful exhale.

I was lost for words. Half because she was taking a interest in me, the other due to my mind going blank as, for a second, I couldn't remember what fake address I'd written on the application for this job. Was she trying to fox me? Or was she genuine? The paranoia you carry around with you in my game, I tell you.

"It's not a trick question, fella," she said. She'd gone back to the first morning, all blasé and impersonal. I much preferred the friendly Melanie of the moment before.

I could hear Dessie's voice buzzing away in my ear telling me not to get too familiar with the mark. But Dessie wasn't standing there at that moment. He wasn't witness to a row of scarlet nails that worked in tandem to flick a cigarette in a way that could only make a fella hanker for more.

"Maryhill," I said suddenly, hoping to fuck it wasn't anywhere near her stomping ground.

To a certain relief, she'd already lost interest in the answer, like you do when someone takes an eternity to reply to whatever was asked of them.

"Ah, bad luck," she said, brushing past me in a way so deliberate I swear there was a static shock running up my arm. Pure electricity.

"Meetin your fella, is it?" I blurted.

"Eh no, nosey parker. If you hang around you'll find out I don't own one of those."

She left me standing there with my tongue wagging like a mongrel.

Day 3

That initial first day, I'd made a list of potential scam scenarios. The till was out, as that was always too obvious with a new employee. Besides, you have to hang around for weeks on end to skim a bit off here and there to total anything worthwhile. And as we've established, *hanging around* just ain't my style. In any case, going for the till is so bloody amateurish. Jesus, I was doing that on the milk floats and paper rounds at age 13. In this gaff, the gold was in the stock. All it needed was a peachy ploy where yours truly would be the least suspected employee because when you've got an alibi the heat never falls your way.

The morning of the scam, I jumped off the bus and made the short walk to the gaff with a right spring in my step. I'd met Dessie the night before to finalise the plans. He'd given me a proper Dessie-style rollicking by suggesting I was a bit too preoccupied with something else. I'd been sharp to shoot down the accusation that Melanie was the reason my head was elsewhere. I'd lied. I couldn't get the girl off my mind. Stacey fuckin McGonagle was like a bad joke in a Christmas cracker compared to Melanie. Of course, I wanted to ride her as soon as I looked at her, but it was something more. I wanted to get to know her, get inside that mysterious and beautiful head, to figure out what makes a girl like that tick.

She'd already taken up her position at the counter a few minutes before opening time. She stood thumbing through a bundle of invoices, just as I'd first found her two mornings before. Looking up softly as I came into her eyeline, she did a double take and I swear a little smile of pleasure rose up on her face when she realised it was yours truly who'd entered the building. Immediately, she tried to suppress it.

But I knew that look, and it gave me a bigger kick than giving that postie a bop ever would. "Well, well. Back for more, is it?" she said, pretending to be all cold and sarky.

"Could be that I'm back for just one thing," I replied. And then I realised there was more to my reply than

I'd intended. Most of the scams in the previous gaffs had resulted in me walking out with a 'prize.' A few along the way had proven too risky, and in those cases, I'd learnt to get out when the odds weren't in my favour. I reckon that's what kept my head afloat—knowing when to deal and when to fold. Following suit along my train of thought, Melanie said, "You play your cards right, and O'Boyle might have you running the place. I know he wants to groom a new right-hand man if it's long-term you're after."

"Did he pay you to say that?" I asked, immediately in bits with laughter. The image of me as O'Boyle's lackey was pure comedy gold. And the thought of my name put in the same sentence as long-term was even more gas. "Anyway," I said, trying to catch breath, "I reckoned *you'd* make a perfect right-hand... man?"

"Hmm," she said with a little snort. Only this girl could get away with snorting twice in two days, and not remind me of an ugly pig. "As you can see, I'm just a female, not a fella—"

"I had noticed," I cut in.

"Had you now?" she smiled, though not so cold, nor sarky with it this time. "And the Pope is just a Catholic too—"

"Really," I cut in a second time, "I was too busy noticing you're not a fella." Could it be, I thought in union with that smile, that this gig actually offered a third option to the equation? What if I actually stayed part of the occupational rhythm for once? What if I actually made a decision to hang around and form a cosy little relationship with Melanie? A lot of actuallys, but still, she could've easily splashed water on me by the third day if she had a *no mixing pleasure with business* policy. Instead, she was giving me the old come on. And then I started thinking in the long term about O'Boyle. A shite like that always has a few dodgy business secrets in the closet. I didn't believe for one minute he'd got to where he was by being even halfway legit. I suppose it was envy that gave way to the idea and motive to do him over on an even grander scale. I was small fry compared to him. But a slice of blackmail, given the opportunity to dig into his books and dealings might just be the challenge of the bigger scam I'd been waiting for. The idea of being O'Boyle's phoney lackey wasn't as poxy as it first sounded. I was sure Dessie would approve too. We'd both been waiting for a big scalp for so long that it was making us itch to the bone.

Just then, a waft of Armani Code filled my nostrils and blanked the cogs of new intentions. O'Boyle came strutting past the counter in his tacky camel overcoat, swinging a bunch of keys around his sausage fingers. Of course, he didn't give a toss that he was interrupting the little *tête-à-tête* me and Melanie had going. He eyed me with a right shifty stare as if he'd just caught me ogling his property.

It was in that moment of his dodgy eyeball falling on me that my decision was made. O'Boyle needed to be taken down a peg or six, and there's no better way to get to a fecker like him than through business and women. I was hatching a plan to get my hands on a piece of both. He may have had his own scheming little idea of shaping me into his skivvy, a titbit of information I already had the upper hand of knowing. It would be a simple case of staying one step ahead of the game. I had to dumb it down, and even force myself into the odd bit of brown-nosing just to make him think that I thought being his lackey was the best thing since sliced Mother's Pride. Plus, whatever was going to develop with Melanie had to be kept on the quiet, though I reckoned that just added another little twist to the game.

Surveying the shop like the lord of the manor, O'Boyle gave a little grunt as he peeled away. "I've a couple of pieces of detective work to do this morning...not to be disturbed."

Right you are Sherlock, I thought, as he walked away, his keys still swinging like he was the warden of H Block.

"Jesus, he's in a right funny one this morning," Melanie sighed, placing the invoices into a folder. "Don't be paying him no heed...but don't go ruffling the feathers either. That's the best advice you'll get today."

Before I got the chance to reply, Morag Aperture came flying past wafting her own ill-fragrance around the counter with the draught of that mink coat. I gave her a wry smile, which she promptly ignored. "Snobby mare," I muttered under my breath. Also giving her a moment's thought, I wondered where she fitted into the whole set-up. If I was to plan on bringing O'Boyle down, the icing on the cake would be to see a right tetchy boot like her go down with him.

"Is he in?" Madam demanded, landing an eyeball on no one.

"Just this very minute, Morag," Melanie said flatly. "Straight upstairs to the office he went."

Morag Aperture practically grabbed the sides of her mink, giving the shop an all-round inspection as she did so. "Right so," she said, as haughty as the Queen on coke.

"I was wrong," Melanie said, her red nails loudly tapping the counter. "The best advice is not to ruffle *her* feathers in the foreseeable."

"What's the deal with her anyway?" I asked, though reluctant to use Melanie as the obvious reference to all the info I was keen to gather. Though by the look on her face, I knew she was ready to dish some dirt if pressed at that very moment.

"She is what ye might call O'Boyle's *slumber partner.* Married into one of the wealthiest business families in Glasgow. God knows why she's got her finger in his crummy pie...though chances are it's the other way about. Even so, it's a bit unusual for her to come in at this time in the morning."

I was champing at the bit to ask Melanie how legit, or otherwise, she knew they were. But I had to be more patient and tactful than that—something I'm not used to. Though I knew I had to learn to deal with both if the prize was to strip the camel off his back and the mink from hers.

Just then, Chubby padded into the shop all flushed and sweaty. He began taking off a huge backpack, followed by an orange scarf, a purple hat and matching gloves with two missing fingers. The sight of him was pure gas as he folded up the woolly paraphernalia into a neat ball.

"You'd think we were living in the Arctic in February, Chubby…" Melanie joked, "it's only October."

"You forget, my dear," Chubby started, "I am from the heart of España, where an average day in October is like the warmest day of June in Glasgow."

"And your point is…?" Melanie smiled kindly.

"…That the weather here is gash!" Chubby grumbled.

We all shared a good laugh, as Chubby's flair for the lingo in his dulcet dialect was as funny as it was dodgy. What is it they call it? Camaraderie in the workplace? Whatever they call it, it was beginning to grow on me.

Just as the hilarity died down, Dessie waltzed into the shop sporting the Glasgow City Council Sanitation Department overall he'd resourcefully acquired, a green baseball cap worn as low as his brow, while carrying three grey sanitary bins. His arrival was earlier than I'd expected, though I knew he wanted the scam done and dusted before anyone knew what had hit them.

I had mixed feelings about the early sight of him. Dessie had been my full-on partner in misdeeds and wrongdoings since we were both tall enough to five-finger discount the merchandise. He'd watched my back and I'd watched his. I'd always trusted Dessie more than anyone, even myself. We couldn't operate without one another, using alternate switches of he being the coalface of the scam, and in this case, vice versa. We'd worked as far afield as Fife and Aberdeen whenever we suspected the heat was on in Glasgow. We were like brothers in terms of having an unspoken rule that if one went down, there was no way the other would follow. We'd cover each other, and take the rap alone if it ever came to it. For the first time in our unillustrious unlawful career, I had doubts about the scam that was about to kick off.

Though it wasn't in terms of fear, or weighing up a sense of bad odds that gave me thoughts of pulling out. It was purely on ambitious grounds. I wanted Dessie and me to take a step up from the ten-a-penny swindles that had barely kept our heads above water. We deserved more. We'd been on the lookout for the challenge of a big one-off fiddle that, if gallus enough, could see us out of Scotland for good. The downside was I decided on the change of tack only in the split second of that moment.

I stared at Dessie as he strolled toward the counter, and knew I'd have to give him a signal. He avoided all eye contact—as was planned—as if I was literally invisible to him. Approaching Melanie, as she glanced at me, meaning I had to avert all my attention away from Dessie, he said, "Here to make my collection, love."

Melanie didn't show any sign that she'd caught me acting like an eejit with my eyeballs, as she asked, "Got some ID there, fella?"

Dessie smoothly placed his bins on the floor and

flashed a badge that matched the alleged exterior of the uniform. She took a moment to stretch over for a better look at the impostor that was Gerry McLeod for his purpose, as I coughed and spluttered and tried to get the signal across. Usually, we'd have a code word at the ready, an indication the heat was on, and so time to abandon ship. But somehow we hadn't prepared one for this scam. Was it too much confidence? Was it complacency? I tried to remember a code word from a previous job, but the only ones that came to mind were the abattoir and the brothel scams when the words we'd used were *pigshite* and *pussy on heat.* Neither seemed appropriate in the moment without rousing suspicion. Like a true, ultimate professional, Dessie didn't flinch a jot. Neither did he bat an eyelid in my direction. I knew then a plan B to abandon plan A was required.

Melanie asked Chubby to take Dessie downstairs and direct him to the ladies' cubicles before I had the chance to get in there and suggest I do that very deed. I was too slow and I cursed myself for it. Chubby, still carrying his woolly gear made his way to the stairs, as Dessie picked up the bins and coolly followed.

Just then as I watched the top of Dessie's head disappear down into the basement, O'Boyle and Morag Aperture came flying out of the adjacent office door. With both their coats flapping like the skins of king-size rodents in midair, they practically galloped towards the counter. His head no longer appeared tantastic orange, more oxblood on fire. Her deep-set laughter lines weren't deep-set by laughter, but through a devilish evil stare I sensed coming my way.

"Somebody's shite's hit the fan!" Melanie said, clearly rattled.

I got the feeling the sight of those two pummelling headlong towards the counter like a couple of fiends was a new sight even to her. "I'd relax, love," I said, with eerie calm, "I don't think it's your shite they're after." I imagined they'd somehow found out about the duplicate Yale, or the Sanitation Department had called to say they were a uniform short, and to be vigilant.

My mind was racing with all sorts of upshots as O'Boyle slapped down a mangled sheet of paper onto the counter with an outstretched arm. The rest of his mammoth body followed as Morag Aperture rounded herself up beside him. I looked down at the sheet lying directly in front of me. It was a copy of the CV I'd used to get my foot into the gaff. All down it in pink and green highlighter pen were crosses and circles over my gleaming previous employment and references section.

Melanie shuffled closer for a good swipe at the sheet. For the first time, I wished she'd kept her distance. I could feel her eyes shift back and forth from me to the circles and crosses. She took a step back, and I immediately wanted her warmth close to me again.

Morag Aperture picked up the sheet like it was a scrap of bog roll covered in crap, as she placed a pair of gold rims on her nose. "Right, shall we start with the most recent pile of shite first, hmm? Three years at Muldoon's in Dumfries? Reputable business that. A glowing reference it seems? Knew Muldoon myself as it goes. Shame he retired and sold up to a florist eighteen months ago though." She peered over the rims with the grimace of a spanked ferret.

O'Boyle practically snatched the sheet from the hand of the devil, as he fingered a circle, his bloodshot scowl burning a hole in my head. "Let's see, previous to your 'three-year stint in Muldoon's' there's a college diploma in retail and commercial management—"

"At North Glasgow College?" Melanie added. I was hurt by her need to join in the nailing of my deception.

"Only problem is..." O'Boyle went on, "North Glasgow College specialises in social care and beauty therapies. Not exactly your scene is it, Lamb?"

"And not exactly the kind of skills required to be part of Pro Photo Inc.," Morag Aperture threw in. "You may have got away with this tripe in other places of employment...the ones too lax in this department for their own good. But your number is up here..."

Blah-di-blah-di-blah was the only thing I heard from Morag Aperture's contorted gob in that moment as I spotted Dessie reach the top of the stairs into the opening of the shop floor, his arms apparently weighted down by the contents of the three sanitary bins. In a fierce quick movement, he looked at me through the frame of O'Boyle and Morag Aperture's wrath. I knew by the satisfied look on his face the collection had been successful.

That pair of shites may have called game's up as far as my 'credentials' were concerned, but as soon as Dessie walked out the gaff and I buttoned up my coat, that I hadn't even taken off, the last laugh would be on those two feckers. Perhaps not the grander scam that could've been, but still the buzz of success in the swindle we'd originally planned from the outset. The Big One would be the next one I decided.

As for Melanie, I felt a bit bollocksed about her. She was a real stunner of a ride, but sometimes all's fair in love and scam, and experience has taught me that the two just aren't born to mix.

I knew my unexpected new role in those next few moments would be to keep the ire of the creature-coated gobshites aimed entirely at my head, as well as keep Melanie's attention completely towards the sheet of deception. Dessie was doing his bit and I was determined to do mine.

I decided to have one shifty last look toward Dessie's stride to scam triumph. As I glanced between *der* brute and the she-devil I couldn't suppress a wry smile. But as I did, I saw Dessie inadvertently trip on the top step of the staircase, his hands not quick enough to halt his mush from smacking against the bannister. In the suddenness of the impact, his arms lost grip of all three bins. The trio of hulking plastic flew into mid-air, fell violently and skidded across the tiled floor at the speed of G-force as Dessie grabbed onto a Fuji promotional banner for dear life. With anticipative horror etched on Dessie's face, O'Boyle and Morag Aperture turned in synchronised shock at the sight of three skanky-lidded containers sliding past their feet, each pouring out boxes of digital cameras, camcorders, quality lenses, memory cards, chargers and a general assortment of Pro Photo Inc. accessories. Melanie and I stretched across the counter in unison for a better view of the scene strewn in front of us. We'd both aimed for the space between O'Boyle and Morag Aperture, and as a consequence our arms and legs became entangled and our heads came to lie within a hair's-breadth of each other. As the trailing goods came to a dramatic stop, Morag Aperture let rip an almighty screech, though I wasn't sure if it was due to the sight of assorted merchandise thudding towards her, or because of the used tampon attached to a packet of AA rechargeables landing on her foot. Either way, a balmy silence fell on the scene, only to be broken by Dessie, entangled in the banner, hopping around massaging a bloodied nose. O'Boyle clenched his fist, now gripped around what was left of the mangled CV, Melanie made a very deliberate move away from my side, as if detaching herself from soiled velcro, and Morag Aperture gave out a second "Eh-ugh!" as she kicked her foot like an epileptic mule.

Amid the commotion, my back started to spasm lying flat out across the counter. Only able to wriggle sideways, what an eejit I must've looked, like a stranded crab caught in a wave of crud. I then felt a heavy hand pin my head against the counter glass. "This is what you might call a citizen's arrest, ya thieving little shite," Morag Aperture announced, applying more pressure. It felt like I was on the bloody rack. "Grab that gouging little bollocks," O'Boyle shouted at Chubby, who'd appeared, throwing himself up the stairs and onto the shop floor like Hong Kong Phooey. Dessie made a woozy attempt at a getaway but ran straight into the custom frame cabinet, smacking his head against a second rail of metal in as many minutes. He spun round a couple of times before crumpling to the floor among the debris he'd just created. Chubby then pounced on Dessie, giving it a right woolly macho pose.

Just then the front door flew open, and in rolled a tartan shopping trolley. Surveying the scene, its owner wheeled herself slowly into the shop. Everyone stopped for a moment at her presence, as the auld dear said in all seriousness, "Could yee all spare a wee minute? I just popped in to see if the Spanish one had been able to process me film?"

In the collision of my tragedy and her comedy, there was nothing left but to laugh uncontrollably.

It didn't help with the bleedin spasm.

Or Blether tae that Effect

So here Ah um sittin in the doactors at quarter tae
eleven fur ma twenty past ten appointment, rubbin ma
cheeks against the fake leather so as no tae use ma
hawns and scratch doon there, when yer one behind
reception oan the phone says, "Is there any chance
Ah kin squeeze ma dug in fur a shave, shampoo and
set oan Thursday evening, whit wae yees bein open
late like?"

The wummin doon the other end must've asked her
whit kind ae dug it wis, cos she goes, "Ma Benji's a
Pekinese, I had him in before. Ah think it wis Miriam
or Muriel or summit that Ah dealt wan time."

Doon the phone Ah kin hear a muffled wee,
"Miriam doesnae work here anymerr, oan accoont ae
the wound no healing and the infection havin spread
upwards."

"Ah see, aye," yer one says, no giein two fucks
aboot Miriam's wound, though it wid hiv been obvious
tae ask how she came by it, wid it no? Mibbaes that's
jist me, cos Ah'm a sick, nosey bastard that wiy.

"So am Ah able to squeeze ma Benji in or whit?
Ah'm no wantin his taes done this time, in case that
comes up oan ma file."

Ah'm wonderin whit the fuck Benji has had done
tae his taenails, and whit else is oan this file...
fur Christ's sakes. The reflection ae her computer

screen is bouncing aff the perspex windae behind and Ah kin see she's oan wan ae they dating sites editing her profile. Maybe she's changing it fae owner of shaved Pekinese tae owner of a shaggy wan wae the canine distress this appointment query is giein her.

"Hiv ye no got a cancellation anytime at aw oan Thursday efternoon?"

In a *if Ah hid a cancellation it wouldnae be a cancellation, it wid be an opening no a cancellation noo wouldn't it* tone of voice Ah kin just make oot the wummin sayin, "Naw, sorry."

Noo the big handsome doactor wae the good skin, bright soaks and broon slips oans has just came striding through the perspex door. The auld wummin across fae me wae the tripod zimmer gies me a look that says Ah hope he rattles her a good wan fur wasting NHS time. Ah nod tae concur.

All thoughts of Benji's shaven bits get thrown oot the windae as yer one jumps up and draps the phone. Wae a thud akin tae a jaggy brick fallin oan her keyboard, she pipes up, "That'll be the doactor fur ye noo, Mrs Wilson."

An awfy awkward silence descends the appointment room whit wae Mrs Wilson havin nipped oot tae the lavvy in the in-between. Ah make a pleadin gurn tae the doactor that in Mrs Wilson's absence surely Ah must be next. Ah mean Ah've got tae be back at the canteen fur noon or big Elsie will huv ma guts fur garters. And Ah huvnae even coonted the veg medleys oot the freezer this morning so that'll be another hell tae mend.

The doactor clearly isnae impressed wae the whole affair as it stauns and whitever flashed up oan the screen ae madam here's dating preferences hasnae sparked him intae fruit-flavoured enthusiasm neither.

There's a bit ae a frosty Mexican stand-aff as Mrs Wilson comes through the toilet door wae her dripping nostril and wan leg shoarter than the other. Another few seconds and Ah wid've been up for ma examination. Ah'm no half burnin doon there and noo Ah'm back doon the pecking order. Christ, Ah'm convinced it's spreadin roon ma back bits noo an aw.

"Izat you ready fur me noo, doactor?" says Mrs Wilson, right oan cue. Whether he wis ready or no, she's set herself headlong through the surgery door like a jakey at an offie closing doon sale. That shoart leg clearly isnae a hinderance tae her.

Yer one behind the desk has been lookin aw sheepish at the phone receiver oan the flair this whole time, as her right hawn noo does a *will Ah, won't Ah* number oan reachin doon fur it. Whit's making her shiftiness merr worse is the wummin doon the other end is giein it, "Are ye still wantin tae book yer dug in then?"

The doactor's held the door open with his long erm and fingers for Mrs Wilson who's bumped his groin as she's whipped past. It wis hard fae this angle tae say whether it wis deliberate or no, but Ah'm giein her the benefit ae the doubt in sayin it wis.

The door's noo shut closed and yer one must think the doactor's gone in efter Mrs Wilson as she's unfroze herself fae the previous state ae sheepy rigidness. Ah kin tell she wis just aboot tae reach doon and pick up the phone, but the doactor wae his long limbs has streeched himself at the waist withoot even bending a knee tae scoop the phone up aff the flair. Aw shaken up wae that wan, she's no realised the doactor wis behind her the whole time. She's gied it a wee jump oot her swivel chair and pit her hawn against her chist like a damsel in distress affy wan ae they auld black and white English films.

The doactor's got the phone in his hawn and puts it up tae his mooth. "Ye better book Benji in at your concession rates..." he says, dead matter ae fact like. "...The wans ye gie tae folk that hiv jist goat their jotters."

...Or blether tae that effect.

It Ain't Easy Being Glasgow's
Most Eligible Gay Woman

On or around public transport have never been places for gay women to 'meet' women—*discuss.*

Okay, I'll start...

One morning earlier this year, the following bus ride became a good case in point.

Of course, (and presumably *off course*) the 8:05am arrived at 08:17, no shock there. As a mathematical side thought, I'm sure I've stood for an accumulative one-fifth of my adult life in bus shelters and another two-sixths aboard double-deckers. Some shitey waste of precious time altogether.

As I boarded my 46 that day, a lassie with a pram came scuttling down the aisle, leaving me with no option but to press myself against the driver's door window, like a slug down a pint glass. Sluggishly, I was beaten to the bit by two teenage lassies who flounced themselves onto the last empty flip-up seats like a set of conjoined twins. Left upright, I moseyed around the pole next to the *Metro* stack trying to look unperturbed. And then she caught my eye. A lovely wee Amy Macdonald circa *This is the Life* look-a-likey, all wrapped up with a thick woolly scarf and a highly-charged smile. I met her gaze twice in rapid succession. There was I attempting to look all über-cool, just me and my pole.

The intensity of the moment was only broken by

188

conjoined high-pitched twitter by way of the teen lassies.

"Am sure I seen that bus driver up the dancing last week," the taller one of them chirped.

"Never seen him before in my puff," her pal shrugged, biting her nails. "Here, did you put the last of your Lanzarote euros in the box?"

"Aye, he was that busy checking me out, he didn't even notice."

"You're full of it, so ye are. I put two of my sunbed tokens in...daftie must really fancy me then."

It was impossible not to turn and catch a glimpse of where these crazy utterances came from. In all the distraction, Wee Woolly had left her seat and was in the process of alighting, before a second head-swivel gave me time to realise. Shuffling away, she left a draft of mystique on the pavement, as my mini prayer was answered in the look-up. Even the condensation on the window couldn't hide that coy little upturn of her lip and twitch of her pixie nose. I gave a double-raising of my eyebrows to suggest *same place, same time tomorrow...8:17am—late but sharp.*

But did I see her the next day, or the day after, or the day after that? Did I bugger... All I was left with was a double-dose confirmo that neither public buses nor train timetable displays are conducive to the cosmic possibility of meeting women within the sapphic range, let alone offer the chance to perfect the art of picking one up.

On a whim a few years ago, I decided to get away by taking a trip to London. I don't know what I was thinking really as it was the middle of November, and too late in the day to sort a flight leaving the same evening from Glasgow—so I hastily got myself booked on the over-night Megabus. Seated and settled, I prayed with fingers literally crossed that no one sat beside me, at least no one weird…

Aaargh, *why always me!?*

His name was Doody or Dodo or some similar daft moniker. He ran his own mobile phone covers racket, gave me a lesson in silicone casings and in the dead of night tried to feel me up with a slimy little hand that was in turn crushed by mine own with more ferocity than a titanium nutcracker.

To this day, I maintain getting touched up on a coach by a woman I even find absolutely repulsive is a ultimate lesbian badge. It's kind of like saying, yes, to women, I'm merely irresistible. You've not lived until you've been touched up by stranger lady fingers after midnight, be that on a Vengabus or Virgin First Class. God loves a tryer, but naturally, Dodo could fuck right off.

No, the cosmos has never been kind to me where moving vehicles are concerned. If a single hot dyke is on the same train as me, the likelihood is she's in Carriage B, while I'm trying to keep myself entertained with sudokus and afternoon Radio 2 in Carriage F. And needless to say, the planets won't be aligned that day, hence our buffet cart and toilet visits will never collide.

In making a stand though, I've decided a way of resolving this whole issue is to purchase a vintage decommissioned London bus, funk it up with a mini bar, a few velour-covered couches, soft lighting and send it on a speed dating tour of the nation's towns and cities with a *For Her Eyes Only* banner on its side. Only then will we single gay women ever be in with a chance of finding someone aboard public transport— *feel up purely optional.*

But it is tough being Glasgow's most eligible gay woman, I kid you not. More than half a million souls live in and around the city. Okay, subtract a quarter of a million with XY chromosomes, right off the bat. Add (nay also subtract) women under 18 and over 50... I'm not ageist, but you (even I) have to make the cut-off somewhere. Subtract the straight women... (there's a famous sapphic joke that straight women are straight...until they're not). But let's face it, there are women in this world who would no more delve into pussy as much as lesbians who'd no more delve onto cock.

Then there's the bisexual ladies, and let me tell you they're more hassle than they're worth. They want the soft, emotional side of a woman, but the rough and the gruff and the body hair of a man, or is that vice versa...? I can never remember, but there's more chance of working out the weather eight weeks on Tuesday than working out which way a bi lady is swinging today.

Now we've all heard that cry of a heterosexual woman...*all the good men are taken, or gay!* A good, wanton lesbian loves a paraphrase, as she shrieks, if I'm not mistaken, that *all the good gay women are*

191

straight...or dead. Sometimes I think it's both as there must be millions of lesbians to who've left this earth never having happily lived and loved as one. *Tragic.*

Anyway, back to crunching the numbers in the pool of the proverbial single-available-unfucked-in-the-head-100%-straight-up-in-their-gayness women out there. At the end of the day all I want is to meet a nice, normal lady who'd be generous with her money, make room for my Dusty Springfield shrine and be happy to wear double denim on our wedding day...make that *quattro*-denim. I just want to take us out of the big dirty pool and into our happy wee Belvadere jacuzzi. Don't get me wrong, I'm no gold digger. I earn my own money from the man and pay it back into the system like most poor sods. And let it be known, I'm not into the latest craze of looking for a sugar mammy. There's a whole generation of over 50s professional ladies (that would've been monikered spinsters back in the day) with their mortgages near paid and no weans nor whiff of an alcohol nor gambling problem to speak of. Their disposable queer pound can keep a few baby dykes in a lifestyle they could become accustomed to. Though true enough, I've been skinto, rooked-a-rama, on my cute, but skinny arse on certain occasions in life. The worse part is when you're a poor gay lady trying to do some impressive romancing. I was really broke one time but wanted to take this girl out on a second date. There we were all smiles in the pub when I asked her what I could get her from the bar. When she said, "Oh, I guess I'll have Champers," I said, "Aye, guess again!"

That's a reminder never to woo a high-maintenance lesbian, skint or not. A thrifty tip for the striving, single baby dyke student is to get a hold of one of those big Havana cigar tubes and fill it with bees. A smashing cost-effective vibrator in summer. But you know you've hit rock botty when you find yourself in the Give Blood Bank just for the biscuits. It was a bit on the cheeky side after flirting with the nurse to leave a note in the suggestion box, which read, *any chance of a dark chocolate coated biscotti next time?*

But we've got it good in Scotland, haven't we? What a wonder the NHS is. I have an American friend. One of those real hypochondriac Californ-I-A types—as American as a cheeseburger in a Chrysler singing *Yankee Doodle Dandy*. She lives by this one thing; if you can't afford a doctor, go to the airport wearing a clunk of concealed jewellery. You'll get a free x-ray, a breast examination and if you mention bomb they'll give you a colonoscopy. She's the best hypochondriac doing the rounds—always got the remedy ahead of the pain.

Once past the dating days (though not past the debt years), it's always tricky that realisation early in a relationship that your girlfriend earns a lot more money than you ever will. Call me bitter, but that stuff really starts to annoy the hell out of you, and every little thing she does simply grates. In your head you're thinking, *check her out, scrubbing the pans of beef stroganoff sauce that she made us for dinner tonight.* And *who does she think she is...going online and sponsoring a barefoot orphan child in the Sudan.*

For the sad lesbian who's acquired one payday loan too many, a surefire money-making scheme, if you have six hours a day put aside for it, is the surveys racket. Surveys 4 U, Survey Monkey, the Survey friggin Bistro! I've done them all. 50 credits per every hundredth morsel of private data given to Big Brother and marketing mad conglomerates, which equates to a free salad at Nandos and one entry into the next *Reader's Digest* prize draw. It's perhaps more tantric a career than quick-fire, right enough. Talking of surveys, they say 4 out of 5 people suffer from their homosexuality. That means one enjoys it...so it may as well be me. And remember the next time a government think tank asks 'what do you attribute your gayness to' give it the straight-up answer... LUCK!

A few weeks ago I received an email which at first glance made the Gettysburg Address look like a scribble on a napkin. It was a reminder, a summons, and an itinerary all in one from the chief bridesmaid of my good friend—a convoluted lowdown on the hen's hoedown, so to speak.

Chomping away at a high-fibre cereal bar at the time—which was easier to digest—there had no hint of inescapable action which might have caused me to shirk...until I read the line, *Saturday night's theme is Superheroes!*

Now let's be clear from the off, if I was to ever make an appearance on the show *Room 101,* going down my chute, just ahead of gherkins and slow motorway drivers would most certainly, definitely and without question be hen parties. You can't turn them down, but I can never truly turn up to one with body and soul fully invested. I knew I was in shtook. I couldn't let down a friend who I'd known since school and no one would believe it if I said it clashed with my summer holiday abroad, not with this one falling on the third week of February.

The thing about a friend's hen party is you end up realising she has more people in her life than you ever imagined. First, there are the girls from her work who form their own wee clique from the get-go and only smile politely at others in the group as a way of joining the social dots. You can tell a couple of them don't get out much and are rubbish at small talk and putting a worthwhile two cents into any chat that doesn't involve the teensy radius of their workplace. Then there's the hen's sister, who is four years younger, was always big for her boots and has done far too well for herself in adulthood, having already wed and set herself up nicely with a four-bedroomed semi in Newton Mearns. With unrepentant sororal rivalry still oozing from her every pore, she pretends that the love and attention should be aimed towards the best big sis in the world, but connivingly it's always all about her.

Then there's a few aunties who spend the night saying how it was so different in their day when lassies used to go out the very night before the wedding rattling pots and pans and selling kisses for 50p.

Between the work colleagues and the aunties, they've heard the rumour that there'll be a lesbian among them for the night. This I've been texted by my pal in the days ahead. "Tell them to be very afraid," I replied. "I'll be wearing a big black dildo attached to the crotch of my Supergirl pants," I warned "They're going to love you," was the reply with a dozen tear-rolling emojis underneath.

One thing the citation had failed to verify and wasn't picked up on in the tortuous What's App group chat was who was wearing what in terms of costume choice. On rendezvousing at the Radisson Blu, where a few of the girls were booked in for the night—what with them living in Airdrie and Lanark and other far-off places—it became apparent that some had gone for the Rolex of fancy dress outfits, whereas others had veered more towards the Gerald Ratner selection. With the exception of the hen striking a stunning pose as a fabulous head-to-toe Wonder Woman and her sister stopping public transport dressed as a skin-tight, oversexed Catwoman, the rest of us looked like dregs in a bad pantomime.

Between the remaining ten of us, there were three Batgirls, a Mrs Incredible, me as Bananawoman, one pink, one yellow Power Ranger, a She-Ra, a Poison Ivy and one of the hen's neighbours had at the last minute pulled together a homemade ensemble that bore a cross between a coked-up Princess Leia and a S&M madame. No one dared asked who she was meant to be without a drink in them.

Once in rank, we were supplied with bright pink

sashes and a willy wand the size of a camping mallet as part of our accessories. As we stepped out into the chilly late afternoon, I was glad I'd been able to fit two pairs of bed socks under my banana skin boots and a mask that fitted enough of my head not to be recognised in public or inevitably across social media.

After the pizza, sausage rolls and shot games, there I was heading into town on a bellyful of Apple Sourz with my lovely lassies, all of them, as far as my gaydar could tell proper common or garden straight types. Not a lager drinker among them, and each over-excited at throwing away ten-quid-a-pop on bucket cocktails to dip their willy straws into.

On we headed to The Merchant on the corner of West George Street with gusto when it occurred to me...yet I had no idea, nobody told me, why wasn't I warned...? Superhero hen's parties are like, well, magnets to real willies...and a few arseholes, period. I'm no expert on cacti but I know a prick from 20 yards, and they were headed our way.

Within half an hour we'd been inveigled by two Irish stag parties and a young farmer's collective from the Borders. Thinking it wise to slip away from the mayhem that was the pub's upstairs make-do dance floor once a few buckets had been downed, no sooner did I look up from a *Proud Mary* vertical arm shake Tina would've been proud of when I realised the young farmers had totally convened around us. Luckily the deputy chief bridesmaid was a dead ringer for Olivia Newton-John in her prime and flaunting her inner Sandy took the heat off a bit.

I switched my gayness up a notch or six—that sure warded off the advances of the thick-necked, Lonsdale T-shirt-wearing one a tad. All at once, the Irish stags appeared wanting in on the action and proceeded to preen themselves and dabble in a bit of body popping across the pub floor.

It all became a bit of a stand-off as the farmers shook their tail feathers to impress us, only to be usurped by whatever the name *is* for lads from County Wexford banging their chests off one another. It's incredible the effect a dozen female superheroes can do to a gaggle of staggers. Never mind feeling like the only lesbian on the periphery of the world amidst the hetero bastion that is the straight pub dance floor. My whole being felt closer to the planet Neptune's gravity pit at that very moment.

...And then it happened, a vision like an oasis in my desert of time that was standing still. There she was, my little Amy doppelganger across the other side of the pub. She stood there as ethereal and too good to be true as she'd done on the 46 bus. I'd searched high and low everywhere across the city with no joy and now there she stood hovering around the spiral staircase of this crazy cesspit of hormones. I'd run through my head a million times what I'd say to her and how I would say it and how she'd laugh with me (not at me) as if it and I were the funniest thing to walk the earth. My heart was beating ninety to the dozen and all of a sudden I felt hot and sickly and claus-trophobic all in the same millisecond. I looked myself up and down, having totally forgot I was bedecked in a yellow banana-esque super crap get-up and matching headpiece. When I caught myself in the mirror I was loath to admit it was akin to a primary-coloured gimp mask. It was not a good look. I'd never felt more unsexy, more uncomfortable in a second (banana) skin in all my days. I realised I'd have to hotfoot it across the pub floor if I was to catch up with wee Amy as she turned and started to make her way down the stairs.

I had to make a decision sharpish...do I run after her in my big banana boots, or do I let her disappear a second time, lost again to the city pavements? It was a no-brainer, and in choosing to bounce out of there I had to slap a couple of farmers out the way a little harder than I knew I had the strength for. With my hens and a muckle of staggers left in my wake, I jumped across the pub three strides to one. There were tables, chairs and more drunk people to contend with but they all seemed eager to give the strident banana a wide berth when they saw it coming towards them. By the time I got to the top of the stairwell, wee Amy had descended and as I looked over the railing I caught the top of her head floating down the last few steps. I half slid, half jumped over the bannister in a mad gangly move, rolling and bumping my way down in perpetual motion. Landing on my arse at the bottom, drunk folk looked on, not sure whether to laugh or help. I made a beeline for the front door and its little stepped vestibule. Out in the February cold, the bite hit me like a Two Ton Tessie across my cheeks. It's incredible how a bitter chill makes you realise just how pissed you actually are. But she was nowhere to be seen. I looked left, looked right, looked left again, like a scene from a Green Cross Code advert. I decided to head up Renfield Street where I dipped in and out of the shady city lanes and rape alleys. *Where had my wee Amy gone?* She'd only had a half a minute start on me and as I scoured the streets in my Bananawoman outfit I had to block out the shouts of "it's a bit early for Halloween, hen" and echoes of "one banana, two banana, three banana, four" as I made a U-turn down Hope Street. *Hope*, ha! I'd all but given up on it. Then I started to think that perhaps my wee Amy was just a mirage in the lonely chambers of my mind, or it was all part of some *Candid Camera* skit to get me running around like a mad yin in this banana attire. By the end of Jamaica Street, I'd truly run out of puff. My costume had got snagged, my gimp mask dangled off my ear and my boots had lost all grip on pavement potholes. I caught sight of myself in a waiting taxi window and had to consider just what wee Amy would have made of this mad woman running through the town after her in this get-up. More chance of being laughed at than with, but God (if she really exists) does love a sapphic tryer.

I'd lost track of how long I'd been looking and before hypothermia hit, I trudged my way back up to The Merchant in a right sorry state. As I rejoined the hen posse they actually welcomed me back into their collective bosom like a long-lost warrior, sharing their concern and mentions of "search parties for one."

My bestie grabbed me in a bear hug and ordered

her sister to get me my own bucket. I didn't have the chance to explain where I'd been for the last hour, but before I knew it, my tropical booze pail had arrived and I had a willy wand shoved in my mouth to help with that.

And do you know what...I'm not even going to go there with the old chestnut *if you can't beat them...*

Cat Cochrane

Union Street Junkie

With eyes down
I know still it's me she's coming toward
I focus on a pavement crack, hoping
it'll swallow either she or I, before she asks
Want tae buy this bus caird?

I'm aware I don the look of *huh?*
the concrete slit getting it
Four days left oan it, gie it tae ye fur a fiver?
The frazzled card gives me license
to quit the crack
Some poor, gold-toothed gypsy glares up,
the hand that carries him
in a state of junkie shake

She has dense capillaries,
that weather-beaten—beaten look
Her jaw hangs like fragile cement,
no rhyme nor reason
to its pendulum swing

Haggling with faraway eyes, she says
Awright hen, call it four quid, know?
All the while the bottom lip seesaws
in tight contorted acts,
a plea that sits with me uneasy

I put her at ten years younger
than the lifeless grey wisps
greased around her ear
—down at the next stop
a co-dependant mirror image shouts
Mon, for fuck's sake...move it!

Comedic and sad,
she bounces away, laden springs
for tiny steps along Union Street
Next patsy approached,
I stand less exposed
and revert back to the crack

Tuesdays

What's the actual point of Tuesdays?
Pitiful nose-picking, arse-end
wee wedge runt
of a nowhere day

Tuesdays be like the invisible man
who's misplaced his powers,
left them in the cludgie
to roll among the skitters

By Tuesday life's sucked out of me,
the same way I sooked
from a frozen quenchy til
all the cola was deid in the dregs

If Tuesday was a baddie in a movie
they'd be kicking an orphaned baby
into a helicopter propellor, the nick of it

They say Tuesday's child is full of grace,
but who wants a genteel, snivelling
wee brown-nosed wean
cutting about their feet?

And should Tuesday have a look on her
it would be the face I make
when it's my round
and some fud orders a double

While the French call their Tuesdays *Mardi*
Perhaps that's Mardi for Mardee Bum
and the Stones' Ruby Tuesday
was always a shite song anyway

Tuesdays were better in the auld days—
my Da says people in Glasgow
had a hauf day on a Tuesday,
cannae even imagine it

Cat Cochrane

She Shoulda Been a Contenda

I knew her when she sang the clubs,
red lipstick spoiled
on spit-stained
microphones

Friday nights were glam,
away from the grime on sweat
monotony of the foundry

Never would she slip her hand
with non-workplace folk,
her callous roughs
kept fists squeezed

But when you sing like she did
people want to take your palm
and pat your shoulder

She would laugh then,
a laugh so loud, that unmistakable
Elkie-esque cackle

Then she ghosted the clubs,
shacked up with *him fae Shotts*
horses, fecklessness, a temper to boot
—neither'd won a watch

Lipsticks left unpacked
from the flit out of town,
skills in the foundry wasted
mopping high school lavvies

She was a contender
in her own lost orbit,
a legend in her own lunchtime

Better than most and husky enough
to belt out *Pearl's a Singer*
for prizes, or mere kicks

She's laid her bed,
sleep in it she'll have to,
hell will no mend him

Old lipsticks in front of the bedroom mirror,
Friday nights, lights, the crowd—
doors bang, bulbs flicker
…horses, fecklessness
          and a temper to boot

Compulsions of a Dumped Man

That most virile of groans, the one I keep especially for when the alarm goes off after what feels like only an hour's sleep is now pitched an octave higher as I whack my hand against Ikea beech. In a perfect world I should smile, my day having already detached itself from the usual groundhog of slamming the clock towards the floor altogether.

But it's not a perfect fuckin world. And surrendering to the ceremonious need, I slam it anyway.

If she'd been lying there next to me, Angie would have given her own wee reactionary grumble. But she's not. And I groan again. Deeper, more muffled. Teeth bitten into the crusty-edged duvet.

That first moment of awakening should be a beautiful thing. It's the tiniest moment of the day when we're conscious, though not lucid. Awake, but still numb. I've always said the moment directly after provides a gauge to my pleasure-o-meter. If I give a salute to that second of coherence, gratified I am about to live another day in this skin, I'm decidedly more or less happy to walk the earth the following 24 hours. However, if I feel immediately cornered by the realisation that it's me, prone and vulnerable, wishing I was in some other luckier bastard's skin, chances are I'm in for a cunt of a day.

Funny thing is, yesterday I was giving it high-five

salutes on a grandioso scale. But yesterday morning...
she hadn't left me, yet.

I've left my watch in the bathroom, and I know
without even looking that the clock has landed outwith
arm's reach, neon numbers faced down, just like the
proverbial open jam sandwich. Of course, this means
I have no concept of time as of ten seconds from now,
so I'm nothing if not likely to just lie here for the next
quarter of an hour pretending only eight-and-a-half
minutes have passed.

The next millisecond is filled with the thought of
phoning in sick. Nothing new there. To that extent,
perhaps today isn't so divorced from any other, after
all. Rolling onto her pillow, it's her shampoo and not
the perfume I bought her for Christmas that prevails
up my nostrils. Is it this, or the fact I know Angie
wouldn't call it *her* pillow that irks me so?

What Christmas had that been? Not the one where
we'd averted comedowns—still dressed as gangsters
from the previous night's fancy dress party—by
popping doved-stamped eccies, together on the
inflatable air bed as though we were the only two
living souls determined not to muster turkey appetites.
The wrath thrown at us by our families due to our non-
appearance was worth it, as the pills kicked in and we
role-played a hold-up in the lounge using Monopoly
money and a kids Tommy gun—Angie the sassy
Bonnie, me the dominant Clyde. I thought I was onto
something as the mix of Es and role-play turned her
on. The way I looked at it, pills and acting out should
be like a puppy...i.e. not just for Christmas. She didn't

see it like that, though. No matter how much I tried to persuade her, she was adamant spontaneity couldn't be re-lived. One-offs, that's what Angie set her stall by. Fuck, how I hate Christmas now.

I wonder if my pillow smells of me. Perhaps just a mirror image of me—apathetically limp in soul by day, eagerly potent in body by night. What a fuckin catch I am. Shame on her for not thinking the same. Aye, okay...I admit it, it's fuck all to do with pillows and pills and puppies...and yet everything to do with it. History, eh? I'll have her know I believe in history...two Christmases worth, and all the bits in between. And now she's saying she wants "a break." A break? A fuckin BREAK? When I was at school and someone said, "Gie me a break, eh!" I always replied, "What do you want first, arms or legs?"

I can't hear the boiler ticking over. Which means Ray's forgotten to set the timer again, Christ, when I get my body out from under this lovely goose-feathered nest it's going to be fuckin freezing, again. Just because his feet won't touch the ground the other side of 6:30am for five hours, doesn't mean he has to go all sadistic and forget to set the bloody heating. It's at this time in the morning that I embrace my resentment for him to the hilt. In many ways, taking it out on him as a lousy flatmate before sunrise takes my mind off...

Right, fuck this shit, I'm up! Where's the light? There's the light. Right, where's my dressing gown? On the floor at the foot of the bed...where you left it, you stupid cunt. The sleeves smell of Herbal

210

Essences...I really should stop putting her shampoo in the conditioner compartment of the washing machine.

I'm up. Aye anyway, at least I'm up. Shouldn't have kicked the jammy clock there though. That thing's seen more abuse than a dedicated traffic warden. I feel like trampling around the flat wearing ski boots and sticking on some thrash metal just to piss Ray off, but that stupid fuck would sleep through an Orange Walk in a thunderstorm. Anyway, I'm too tired. I'm going to leave the bathroom light off until I've had a piss. So fuckin tired, I am. It's that tired way you get, you actually feel physically sick. The smell of toothpaste never helps. Shit, I'm pissing over the rim. Can't see it, but a bloke can always sense a wayward trajectory. She wouldn't have laughed if I'd said that to her. Ha! No, Angie would be the last person on earth to laugh at that. I suppose, to the female form, morning urine on the pedestal mat is no laughing matter regardless of...well, piss all.

What's the time now? Is it past the eight-minute warning? Okay, let's chance the light. Why can't they put dimmers in bathrooms as standard building procedure, for Christ's sake? Blimey, I look a pure shambles. My teeth look grey in this fluorescence. I never noticed that before.

It looks like I'm losing my eyelashes. I remember pictures of me as a wean, and I'm sure I had a cracking set of lashes...in fact, I remember women coming up to my Ma in the street and saying so. Oh, hasn't he got eyelashes any lassie would kill for? Is this the first sign of the onset of alopecia?

211

A man with practically no eyelashes, eh? That's gonna look really bloody stupid. It's up there with albino features, just plain unusual looking. But worse, because folk won't be able to take their eyes off something that's not there, no fuckin lashes. Maybe it won't be too bad...the Mona Lisa has no eyebrows and not a lot of folk notice that.

I did though, when we visited the Louvre. My first stab at romance that was—booking a Valentine's weekend for me and Angie in Paris. Fuck it's freezing there in February. Paid through the nose too. She got so drunk on classy vino that first night she couldn't, well...perform. All that layout, and no fuckin return. I should've smacked myself over the head there and then, if only I'd realised it was a sign of things to come.

Thursday today. It might as well be Tuesday. Man oh man. Right, here goes. Positive thoughts before I start thinking about what that shithole has in store for me today...aye, ehh...

It's my birthday! Well, a week today it's my birthday. And in one week and a year from now, I'm supposed to be in Rio. Belter thought that one, doing the Copacabana. Not that I'm ever going to be in Rio, though. Who's kidding who...? Aw that's right, I'm kidding me. That's right, what's new?

My big Four-O it'll be. I'm starting the countdown to it, as of right now. It falls on a Saturday. Somehow I feel lucky my milestone should fall on the best day of the week. It would've been a Friday, but next year is a leap year.

When was the last time I was lucky? I do that sometimes. I make a thing seem lucky, and spin it around. God knows, who the fuck wants to turn—or looks forward to turning forty? I've got to put some positive spin on it. Just like pretending I'm ever going to be sipping Brahma while watching the girl from Ipanema walk by. Still, a one in seven chance to have a birthday, any birthday fall on a Saturday. Favourable odds? What if my birthday next week fell on a Friday? Then I'd totally miss a Saturday birthday altogether for another, what, seven years? God, I think about such shit when I deprive myself of zzz.

Note to self; buy a new toothbrush. No wonder my teeth look the colour of putty. One time I used Angie's electric toothbrush. I laughed out loud when I actually started brushing my cheeks, chin, and eyebrows with it. Quite comforting that tickly sensation. There'd been the impulse to tickle my ear wax with it too, a temptation that merely foreshadowed the weird impulses of a sick man. And so now, is it bad karma? Is this sudden case of bad dentistry another example of her holding a non-providential sway over every degree of me?

I need a coffee. Better still, I need a drink. A two-scoop Irish Coffee with heaps of sugar, what a champion of breakfasts that would be. But there's no whiskey, and I'll be lucky to open the fridge and find milk, never mind whippy cream. Passing the spare room on the way to the kitchen, the dawn chorus of Ray's snoring feels like the only sound resonating within a five-mile radius. Stupid bugger's never laid a finger on a snooze button in his sorry life. I flick on the boiler, to both heat this igloo and allow the radiator clicks to drown him out. A flatmate he isn't really. I remind myself one of those contributes by sticking money in the kitty, doing the dishes, never leaving manky socks on the draining board and so on. Aye, Ray's fucked up inverted sense of contribution is to not set the heating timer, reminding me to thank him when the leckie bill is low after a winter of cold showers. Saying all that, I must be a king-size mug for letting him away with all his shit.

Okay, I really have no concept of time now. Moseying back to the bathroom to collect my watch, it's 06:46 and I'm not showered. Time waits for no man, as they say. Lifting the watch from the sink, I place it in my dressing gown pocket.

She'll be on the last stretch of her night shift now. But sometimes it doesn't work out like that, eh? Like when you suppose all day where a person is alleged to be, or where you expect them to be—but then you find out later they had the day off work, or a doctor's appointment, or a team building faff-about in the Highlands with paintballs or something. And when you do find out, somehow your mind's eye feels cheated because you'd spent all that time supposing the wrong thing. But then, I never thought in those kinds of ever-decreasing circles until I met Angie.

I've decided not to switch the radio on. Instead, I flick the standby on the TV remote and press the red button for the weather report. I know the buttons on my remote off by heart, even in the dark.

I don't know why I look at the national reports first. It's not as if the rain in Redcar, the wind in Wrexham, or the fuckin sleet in Slough is going to make a difference to my day. I think it's my compulsion to see the bigger picture in all things. I switch the page to the local weather—heavy rain in the west spreading east, winds easing in the afternoon. Don't know why I look at any of this bullshit at all. I only have to look out the window to see what shitty kind of day it's going to be. In fact, I only have to live in Scotland to know what the weather's going to do at all. Though I do wonder about meteorological elements. Like later on, is Denmark or Norway going to get that heavy rain, a nice little donation from us? Here you are Mr Viking Man, have a lovely wee precipitable present from your not-so-fair-weathered friends.

Am I hungry? It's last night's curry or mouldy morning rolls if I am. Funnily enough, I decide I'm not. What if she's not on the ward? Wednesday night shift...she should be. But what if she's not? Where would...no, where *could* she be?

I do, I mean, I really do try not to revert everything back to begrudgement. But, it's on the whole, inevitable. Inevitable along with the baggage, the exes...the doctors that roam about that hospital thinking they're George fuckin Clooney. "We should've met when we were fourteen," I said, after a few at her work's night out. "Angie...don't you think? I mean, if it had been that way we wouldn't have spent so much time filling in the gaps." She gave me a look that suggested she wasn't in the mood to read between my lines. "Let's face it," she said, not even looking at me, "some of us are more obsessed with filling gaps than others."

Somehow remembering that automatically lands me onto sex. Well, not sex, per se. More like no sex, per se. I held out for 66 days, believing her to be worth it. I convinced myself I was in love with Angie after only eleven head-spinning days and nights. Not earth-moving, mind, just bloody head spinning. I put it to the back of my mind, and my loins, that after four dates to the cinema, two Indian takeaways, and the third DVD night at hers, she gave in by way of pity, not lust. Weak, inattentive lovemaking from Angie was better than zilch. Six months later, Ray bought me a birthday card with the punchline, BAD SEX IS BETTER THAN NO SEX! The whole thing made me decidedly squeamish. One, for the fact that fuckin card sadly summed it up, and two because Ray had guessed enough about the sorry state of my sex life in the first place. Begrudgement, anxiety...anxiety, frustration... along with Ray, the almighty banes of my life.

Suddenly I've gone from the weather report to the tumble drier, the impulse making me strangely dizzy in the process. My uniform for the shithole is laid out in the bathroom, where it's always kept overnight. But that's by the by, I've decided. Raking through the worn dish towels and damp boxers, I pull out clean jeans and a weekend shirt. Sick bastard I am, sniffing the denim crotch, just to smell her.

Lashing it back into the bathroom, I don't feel so tired anymore. The water is now just the warmer side of tepid. I let it run, and eye my uniform; stiff navy blue flannels with frayed hem, and faded navy polo, lacquered in white deodorant stains. How I hate that stupid costume—the shirt so faded it doesn't match the shade of the flannels anymore. Gathering the two-piece up into a ball, and throwing it out the bathroom across the hall into my bedroom, I've decided, seems the best place for it. Peering through two doors, the polo is sprawled over the clock in the corner—both artefacts now, a disservice to my state of mind.

A three-minute shower is sufficient—razoring growth, polishing putty, cleansing crack. As some blokes might say, the most productive three minutes of the day. On go the jeans and shirt...on a Thursday too. I laugh. Though fuck knows why. I feel like writing HELP! with my finger across the steamed-up mirror. Should I have seen it coming? She'll say I should have.

I take my watch from my dressing gown. Exactly one hour til she'll feel the morning air again. I knew it was serious...well, I knew I was serious by the twelfth night when I started to think about what Angie had been doing all her life, while I'd been plodding along with mine. I quizzed her to recall what she'd been doing the very moment I'd won my 200m race at the school sports day, or what had been on her mind the split second I lost my virginity, or completed my first snowboarding run. I'd supplied dates and times and everything. Of course, she'd been so blasé. "Oh, probably just on the toilet, chopping a cucumber and breaking a stiletto heel," she replied. That was so

217

typical of her, diminishing the importancies of my newly-found romantic brain. "Don't knock it," she scorned, "those happen to be monumental moments of my life, too." And so it was with Angie. She'd unknowingly collaborated in opening up that quixotic side of me—equivalently tearing strips from it at every turn.

I nip back to the kitchen, boil the kettle and cut the mould off the morning rolls. Sticking yeast in the toaster always seems to stem that fungal taste. I'm still not hungry, but two scoops of unmilked caffeine and a couple of toasted rolls spanked in Nutella will give me the buzz I need to do, what I've decided, I need to do.

The first chink of light is peeping through the blinds. Looking down onto the street, I spot the guy who works for the cleansing. I see him in the pub, always a Friday, wearing that same standard issue oversized clenny jacket. I've seen people's faces grinch even before they get a whiff of him. Sometimes I pass him on the street on the way to work...but not today, Jose. Now I feel even more sorry for the poor bugger, standing here somewhat at ease in my sudden shift from the norm. Today is likely to be as forgettable for him as yesterday and the day before. Poor bloody sod. Strangely though, peering down on him as he shuffles out of sight, he just might be the luckier bastard's skin I'd prefer to be in today.

A bloke questions more about himself when he gets dumped than when she says yes to a first date. My Dad never gave me advice on this kind of shit.

Though that was his way, and I still looked up to him. *A Man's Man*, that was my Dad. I've tried to pay homage to him, by attempting to give the aura—as he did—of Clint Eastwood or Charles Bronson, always believing any show of insecurity and self-doubt to be no-go signs of weakness. Died a sad, lonely death my auld Dad. Angie trying to say something when she left one of her magazines deliberately open on some garbage titled *Modern Men for a Modern Era* only a few days after the funeral was harsh though. Totally insensitive she is for a bloody nurse sometimes.

Dressed and caffeined, I've scrambled to the CD drawer with one album in mind. Finding it, I remove the casing, give it a blow and place it into the player. Cranking up the volume after pressing the repeat album function, I reach for my keys. Leaving the lounge door wide open, and doing the same with Ray's door, I feel nicely overawed by a calm malevolence. As I step into the outside landing, Iron Maiden kicks in. Cracking up I am at the thought of Ray jumping out his pit thinking he's an extra in a *Hammer* fuckin *Horror* just as Bruce Dickinson starts really giving it laldy. What's more, I'm thinking when was the last time I ever smiled leaving the flat at this ungodly hour? Fuck knows why I'm smiling, though. Aye anyway, fuck him. But, in a funny...no, sick...no, bloody twisted way, I'm jealous of the lazy cunt. This is definitely an aberration-and-a-half day for me to admit that, even to myself. But there Ray is with a wife, albeit estranged on very dodgy terms, and two daughters. His relationship with all three is, granted,

219

on shakier ground than the San Andreas fault—but still, he's been a father, a man of children. He made two babies. He must've been happy, they all must've been happy, at one time. His girls are of him, of his flesh. Presently engulfed in three relational schisms of his own doing is better than having no child of your own flesh. "Me, bitter?... Neither am I misogynist, just because I hate women," I've heard Ray say on numerous occasions. And "If only I'd been blessed with two sons instead, what a difference that would've made." The only book Ray's admitted to reading is *Men are from Mars, Women are from Venus*—what's more making sense of each and every chapter, determined too, that he could add a few of his own. Yet, that angry sex he gets following another blazing row with his ex, and the pureness his daughters' eyes hand him on occasion is enough to keep the stupid bugger on the right side of sane. Bitter about general feminine wiles he may be, but altogether genuinely loveless, he's not.

Angie loves kids. She works on the paediatric ward, so Christ knows it would be weird if she didn't. Though, it's funny that, how she stuttered and stammered when I asked her one time what her preferred baby names were. Did she think I'd jump her bones, wanting to impregnate her the minute she gave the answer of "any...except...Chloe or Jack."

It's the usual cold slap across my face as I reach the path between the flats and the old lockups. That murky silence too, with the sense that the world's not quite awake yet. But I'm more aware of the earth's time zones than most folk. I mean, there's over a billion people apiece in China and India these days, and it's now afternoon in Beijing and Delhi, so the whole world ain't exactly in a fuckin slumber.

Though when the ground feels as still as dead bones, and the only sound is that of water down a runnel or the hum of a distant taxi meter, my footsteps feel like those of the loneliest man on earth.

This morning I'm feeling just that, but with a double almighty whammy and a cherry on top.

I should've grabbed Ray's car keys for the JVN, a.k.a. *the jalopy Volvo number.* I prefer to call it the DTC, (death trap city) on bare bloody swivels. Either way though, if I got behind the wheel, one, no all three, emergency services would have to be put on full alert; the polis due to the fact I don't officially hold a driver's licence...the fire brigade because of the risk of spontaneous combustion as soon as second gear kicks in...and two ambulances due to the likelihood of the fucker spinning off the road into a bus shelter. In saying that, that wouldn't be a bad way to get my arse to the hospital. Angie's ward is two down from the A&E. Parked outside will be the pride and joy, her Mini Cooper soft top.

It's not right for a man to be envious of his woman. Name me a man who's ever openly admitted to that. He'd have to be one of those namby-pamby, new age types—the kind who stay at home with the weans teaching them how to finger-paint and make paper lanterns and all that carry on. Though envy is just as caustic as the begrudge. Two branches of the same

221

tree I reckon. Throughout our relationship, if I heard Angie say, "Oh, my career this, and my career that," once, I heard it umpteen times. Nursing is nursing to me. We all need them at one point or another in our lives. But it's not exactly like being a cardiologist or a brain surgeon, is it? Come to think of it, she didn't take too kindly to that point neither. One of Angie's traits is she treats every walk of life on par with the next. She's the most indiscriminate person alive. It's taught me a thing or two. But I'll never admit that. I'd never admit that she's taught me more than I have her.

As it is, I give the bastarding banger a dirty look as I contemplate the two-mile trek to say what I've got to say.

When I see her I'll make a joke she won't get. But even when she does, she won't find it funny... not when I ask, "what do you want broke first, arms or legs?"

The Collar

Dublin, St Patrick's Day, 1997

Standing, staring at the collar in the sun, engulfed by the crowds' whooping, hollering delight of the parade, the two Dubliners assumed Erin Nash was Catholic. She wasn't going to put them right.

She had tried it though...to get enrolled that is. Firstly enquiring in the September, she guessed Father Dooley was suspicious of her motives, though the meetings and bible readings were his test of her. Just as well she was a voracious orator of the gospels. She loved reading the pages out loud, her voice tilting high and low, putting on a Scouse accent for Peter, a Geordie one for Matthew, and a pure dead Glaswegian number for the Big Man himself.

To her surprise, she was given a devout sponsor by the November, and was invited to the house of Sister Bridget, who didn't dress like a nun, and liked to sit way too close, wafting a breath so sour it made Erin wince. Just because her tongue isn't meant for a round of tonsil tennis doesn't mean she should give a wide berth to a swig of Listerine, she remembered thinking.

It wasn't that Erin didn't want to be Catholic—fact was, that year she really did. She wanted to be part of the intrinsic funky smell of mass, to take part in

223

communion and see what it was like to sit with the body of Christ inside her.

And then there was her main motivation...to feel something of a *bona fide* Celtic supporter. "You can't be a real one of us unless you know the Hail Mary backwards," she was once chastised. "Any Proddy can learn the Hail Mary...actions speak louder than words," was a further implication.

For some time, Erin decided that she had something to prove, and more urgently some proving to make. Though, in the end, as was the reason for a trail of all unfinished business in her life—the commitment, or lack thereof, resulted in her head never being dunked by Father Dooley the following Easter. For her to commit to two slices of toast was an achievement on the periphery of personal obligation, in other words, a step too far.

So when they assumed she was Catholic, Erin didn't let on that she'd attended a Protestant, *ahem*, non-denominational new town school, all the way through her primary and secondary years.

The taller, wiry one of the northside Dubliners called himself Colm and had deliberately failed to introduce his sidekick. The latter butted in regardless and gave the moniker of Beamer. Colm revelled in revealing the name stemmed from his tendency to turn red at the slightest embarrassment. Poor guy could've heated up a vacant room the way his cheeks burned even at the mere mention of his bodily quirk. Erin tried to sympathise.

Oh, father why are you so sad
 On this bright Easter morn'
  When Irish men are proud and glad
   Of the land that they were born?

She didn't know their names before sharing with them a rousing rendition of *Boys of the Old Brigade* while refusing to admit it was the window of Frazer's Pub that did the job of holding her up. After a full breakfast, four pints of Carlsberg and half a pack of Silk Cuts in Paddy's sun, she was happy to be casually propped up. It's a curious thing, how the rules of touch with practical strangers turn on their heads when singing in shape formation, in this case, a triangle. It seems perfectly natural to grab onto another's upper body parts quite vigorously, and if left with bruising so be it. And Erin was. When Beamer ineloquently pelted out *where are the lads who stood with me when history was made* only her shoulder blade knew it was turning black and blue.

A group of Italian tourists turned their eyes from the parade in their direction. "You're gonna see a lot madder shit than this today, *ciao bella*," Erin shouted at the cluster of sleeping bag-clad youngsters.

"Ya mad ting ya," Beamer shouted, egging her on with a bump of his shoulder. Wanting a piece of clout, Colm divulged, half whispering in Erin's ear. "I've got connections with the Ra in Dundalk ye know."

"Who you trying to impress?" she replied, gently nudging her elbow into his scrawny ribs.

"With a brass neck and singing voice like that?"

Beamer chipped in. "Impressive's not what I'd be callin it."

"Shut it, Glow Boy," Colm scowled. Turning to Erin, shielding his body from Beamer, he continued, "You know, it's a pleasure for me, what with your stance being stauncher for the cause than most women. But what I mean is most Irish girls, well the ones we know, don't give a bleedin bollocks about a united Ireland. And well, you just don't seem the type...no offence and all."

"None taken, my weary Provo," Erin assured, giving Colm a look straight down his eyeballs. They stood trying to figure each other out for a moment. "There's nothing round here that's going to ruffle my feathers," she added. Switching a newly lit cigarette to her left hand, she genuflected with all the duplicitous conviction she owned. Hunching her shoulders, she passed the cigarette back, winking at the both of them. "Know what I mean?"

"Ya little beauty," Beamer piped up. "Love it when we're all singing from the same page." His face remained flushed, presumably though from satisfaction.

And there you have it. With one swift hand to forehead, hand to breast, hand to left shoulder, switch to bruised shoulder, Erin was in their club. And so there she stood, upright and proud in her mock glory.

It was Beamer who'd spotted the collar first. His expression turning a spumy canvas of fiery crimson, as he said, "Unless my eyes are feckin deceiving me, that's a bleedin Rangers top that fella's wearing..."

Colm and Erin stood immediately erect.

"Bollocks..." Colm dismissed in disbelief, "who the feck would have the sheer audacity?"

"That little gobshite right there," Beamer pointed, his arms horizontal and index fingers aimed forward. Erin turned to zone in on the trajectory of Beamer's digits, not quite believing it to be true. She stood on tiptoes to improve her vista. The glare of the sun was strong, and with blurred vision the scene was an array of bouncing heads, waving tricolours and little fireballs being pumped in all directions by one of the passing parade floats. Beamer's arms didn't dip from a ninety-degree angle away from his body, apparently determined not to do so until Erin and Colm spotted his fixation.

Frustrated, Erin wished the crowd would part like the Red Sea to give her a clearer view of their alleged perpetrator. And then, *bish, bash...almighty bosh*. If such a heinous act had panned out in front of her eyes outside any other pub, on any other street, on any other day it wouldn't have seemed so holy sacrilegious. But there, on O'Connell Street on St Patrick's Day, not twenty-five feet away from their trio of permeating stares stood a singular lad, dressed in trendy runners, jeans and a zipped tracksuit top. A lad not particularly exceptional from any other—except for one attired misdemeanour.

"Jaysus," Colm spat. "He is. And it feckin is, you know—"

"Feckin little orange bastard," shouted Beamer, waving a fist as red as his mush. An empty bubble

227

hung in the air waiting for Erin to fill it with it with her own reactionary verbatim. "Aye bloody cheek, where the fuck does he think he is, the Shankill?"

There they stood, three offended souls flared up by the insolence of one human being, spotted among thousands, wearing an upturned collar of blue, white and red laying a hefty blot on their Paddy's celebrations, where their only accepted colours were exclusively green and white.

"You're at the wrong feckin parade, ya bastard," Beamer shouted. "It's no the bollocksin 12th July."

A few of those standing around them looked up from their pints, and the Italians started staring again. But the collared one was oblivious to it all. Erin realised he was standing just out of earshot. He stood in the same spot for a few minutes, hands in tracksuit pockets, bouncing up and down trying to get a better view above the six-deep hedge of bodies between him and the passing floats. Erin didn't dare take her eyes off him, for what reason she wasn't entirely sure.

Without peeling out of her momentary tunnel vision, Erin slowly sipped her beer and dragged at her cigarette, aware that she looked robotic in motion. She felt a sense of seething anger rise up her throat into her mouth, creating a horrid acidy boak. Big gulps of warm Carlsberg weren't for soothing her gullet with immediate effect. She heard Colm and Beamer muttering something, leaving her conscious of the fact their interest in the collared one hadn't subsided.

Colm pulled a Dutch Gold brazenly from inside his

jacket. Tapping the top of the can, he leaned over to Erin. "We've made an executive decision," he said, "...when he moves off, so do we." Pouring at a bad angle into his plastic pot, he asked, "You in?"

Erin's strained eye muscles turned, and her head followed. Just by glancing at Beamer, she caught sight of a wound-up edgy expression that mirrored her own. Colm was the calmer of the two, though she knew that air of malevolence when she saw it.

"I'm in," Erin answered forcefully. "Too damn right am in."

Standing together, they'd made their pact. On another day, it may have seemed all too bizarre, as Erin really didn't know those two from a couple of Adams–and yet, she knew their kind well. There were plenty like them to be found in the pubs she'd been frequenting, and the marches she'd been attending. An opportunity may never come along again. Beamer was right, it was great to be reading from the same page—albeit, implicit perusing.

"You can't walk down a street in your town with a Celtic top on," Beamer croaked with husky spleen, fist still pumping, "...and not get harassed."

"It's true," Colm verified with oozing rightousness. "Anytime he goes over for a match...always comes home with a dirty big shiner and a burst lip or two."

Happy to accept their words as gospel, Erin concured, "Aye, and for me, it's the flip side. I love how I can walk head-to-toe in green down any street here...and not so much as a dirty look."

"The feckin little bollocks is on the move," Colm

229

interrupted. Him being a foot taller than most folk was a benefit in the ensuing situation, using his height as a periscope.

In the haste to commence their shadowing, the three of them almost fell over each other aiming for the same opening in the crowd. As Beamer's bulk was not to be messed with, Erin backed off, leaving Colm's gangly legs to almost buckle. With the Italians still staring at them, it must've looked slapstick, Gaelic style.

Colm was determined to play leader as he used all his slight might to get around the front of Beamer, who'd started with a good impression of Ram-Man. Erin could just barely see the top of the collared one's head as he shimmied sideways among the throng. The crowd was getting thicker as they moved toward the middle of O'Connell Street rambling on like foxes eager to keep sight of the prey.

Erin threw out a few "excuse us" and "sorrys" to innocent bystanders as a way of an apology for crushing toes during their intrepid stampede. Suddenly, Beamer halted without warning, causing Colm to attempt a leapfrog over a boy holding an ice cream cone.

"Ya stupid big feck," shouted the boy's mother towards Colm, laying a few whacks on thick with a green jester hat.

"All right, missus," Colm exclaimed, "ye could have an eye out with one of them bells."

Aiming to bring a halt to all the faffing. Erin decided to jump ahead calmly, hoping her accomplices would follow suit, and resemble something less like the *Keystone Cops*. Seemingly keen to follow her lead, she was happy the pursuit turned more composed sharpish. She anticipated the collared one's crossing of Cathal Brugha Street as he pulled away from the street bustle and stopped to light a cigarette on the corner. Erin held Colm and Beamer back, suggesting they wait on their side of the road to avoid getting too close. They aimed for the same lamppost to hide behind.

Lighting her cigarette without taking his eye off Erin, Colm asked, "So tell me this. How exactly does a lassie end up like you?"

"Believe it or not, he means that as a compliment," Beamer winked with his right eye. The other eye appeared levelled on the opposing corner as if he were experiencing strabismus.

"She's not daft," Colm grunted. "She knows what I mean."

"Well," Erin started, feeling the need to pull out a bit of the dramatics. "I'll tell you since you ask so keenly. It's a bit like a big pot of homemade soup..."

Colm and Beamer looked at each other and shared a half-shrug.

"Imagine," Erin continued, "your mostly Protestant-populated town is the carrot—"

"Cause they're orange?" Beamer interrupted.

"I fuckin hate carrots, too," Colm nodded.

"Aye, good one," Erin grinned. "And then you've got your potatoes reflecting your wholesome Catholic education...which plays out, bucking the trend of the oppressive majority."

"Of course, of course," came the reply in unison. It's amazing what these two will believe, Erin thought, as is the trait of all humans to believe what they want to believe.

"Please don't let Brussel sprouts be Celtic," Beamer pleaded, "they're my least favourite food."

"Who the fuck puts Brussel sprouts in a soup?" Colm snorted.

"Well they'd ruin a good feckin story too," Beamer argued.

Continuing unfazed, Erin said, "No, Celtic can only be spinach...not another usual soup ingredient I grant you, but…"

"This is one of they metaphorical-whatsit soups," Colm said, retracting from his previous contention about Brussel sprouts. "So you can put what the feck you like in it." Turning to Beamer, he added, "You could put in a feckin great elk if your little heart desired."

"Don't be listening to that eejit," Beamer nodded. "Crack on."

"Apart from the obvious connection in colour and all," Erin said. "Celtic is spinach as it's your link to strength and heartiness, and is good for getting rid of all those nasty wee toxins, resulting in a general wellbeing of the body and soul."

"Aye, and you know who spinach's biggest fan was?" Beamer chipped in.

"Go on…" Colm spat.

"Popeye feckin Doyle!" Beamer exclaimed. "See,

even he knew...Up the Ra!"

"Up the Ra!" laughed Colm.

"I'll third that," Erin said, chinking what was left in her Carlsberg to their Dutch Golds. She had them on a leash. Erin reckoned that whatever spurious claptrap she gave them in that moment would only add fuel to their already inflated notion of being casualties of browbeaten oppression. "Well, now we come to those little ingredients..." She pinched her thumb and forefinger as if salt were between them, "that don't necessarily add to the nourishment of the meal and most definitely leave an aftertaste. Firstly, the addition of a cup of lemon juice, reflecting a stepfather who hasn't stepped into a church for 30 years, masquerading as a Protestant defender of the faith."

Colm looked pensive, Beamer stood entertained.

"What else, hmm..." Erin took a minute to prolong their anticipation. "Oh aye, a scattering of out-of-season blueberries, that every other day shout *Fenian Bitch* from school bus windows and sports pitches throughout childhood!"

"Really is like Belfast eh," Colm said, shaking his head.

"...Without the bullets and bombs," added Beamer, with a mouthful of phlegm and beer. At a point of sheer vexation, he shouted, "Fuck the Crown!" A hint of bubbly mucus hit the pavement with it.

"That's true," Erin smirked, feeling highly amused. "But you know, the psychological stuff can maim too. Don't get me wrong, if it was the choice of Glasgow or Belfast to live in, that would be no contest. But all the shit that goes on in the West of Scotland can really fuck a person up."

"That mental soup ain't tasting too feckin good right about now," Colm said, taking a swig of beer.

"Enough to be choking on, I'd say," added Beamer.

"Well, it is as it is," Erin said. "And you know what? I wouldn't have had it any other way, as all roads have led me right here...into the company of you two eejits."

"Oh ya cheeky wee feck," Colm cajoled.

Revelling in her soup analogy, as impromptu as it came, it surmised the elements in Erin's life that had brought her to that very point. While she didn't consider herself a victim of her upbringing, in a second of deliberation, she decided that a lifetime of living in the West of Scotland had nonetheless been detrimental. It left her to wonder, what other fucked up spot on earth would prime someone into taking the fallacious stance of a Catholic underdog.

She realised she'd arrived in Dublin to receive affirmation from mindsets like Colm and Beamer that her way of thinking was bang on, and the bilious curse of West of Scotland culture was no longer a reality, now she'd escaped from it. She felt free to indeed walk down O'Connell Street head-to-toe in green. Free to genuflect in a harmonic triangle. Free to sight poetic justice on the likes of the collared one...all without reprisal and retribution, or being brandished a bogus worshipper of the Pope. What's more, she considered herself blessed to be given an opportunity like the very one that lay ahead. Looking up, Erin stood in awe of the Dublin city sky, not a cloud could be seen and the hazy air soaked with zeal and fervour.

"Sun shines on the righteous," Beamer said, overlapping Erin's thoughts.

"Right, game on," she replied in agreement.

The collared one flicked his cigarette to the ground and motioned away slowly into the crowd. Erin, Colm and Beamer moved across the street to continue their pursuit. The lads seem content to let Erin go a step ahead, perhaps realising a female leader of sorts is less conspicuous. She sensed their mutual readiness to follow her all the way down to O'Connell Bridge and beyond, if necessary.

Suddenly, the collared one took a determined left into Cathedral Street. Erin looked behind to gauge the faces of her accomplices, their respective smug grins suggested a satisfaction with that development.

Turning into the short thoroughfare between Marlborough Street and O'Connell Street, the route acted as an oasis from the populated mayhem behind them. Like many roads and alleys of Dublin's city centre in the late 90s, it was strewn with construction wares. A rusty skip sat in the middle, surrounded by scaffolding and meshed tarpaulin hanging from above. The general debris of empty beer cans and cigarette butts added to the grime of the place. The collared one ambled along the pavement in the direction of passing the skip.

In a flash, Beamer ran past Erin and Colm onto the road, halting just short of the big rusting bin. Colm followed sharply, his bony physique giving him a look of lanky absurdity. Tracking them with her gaze, Erin made her own way ahead. She decided to keep to the pavement as opposed to Colm and Beamer, who'd reached the far end of the skip.

Pulling out a Silk Cut, Erin realised she needed impeccable split-second timing for the plan to commence. On reaching her deduced stage mark, "Hey," she shouted, "sorry to stop ye and all, do you have a light there?"

The collared one turned to Erin without stopping, and mumbled something she didn't quite catch. Walking in time with her slow pace, he reached into his tracksuit pocket, momentarily fumbling around. He pulled out a silver-plated Zippo and handed it to Erin. She assumed he was more trusting of her honest face than he should've been. For a second he was forced to halt his steps as she stopped in her tracks just shy of the end of the skip.

Perfectly on cue, Colm and Beamer jumped out of nowhere, immediately pouncing. Erin stood back, still holding the Zippo. She lit her cigarette while she watched the collared one being smothered by Colm's gangliness combined with the hulk of Beamer coming at him from all angles. The overhanging tarpaulin and metal scaffolding acted as a convenient visual shield from potential witnesses.

Spreading her arms around the fracas, Erin marshalled the jostling bodies into Thomas Lane, running back up towards Cathal Brugha Street. The narrow, deserted alley was bereft of all life bar the essence of vermin, fornication and days-old piss. Beamer was artfully brusque with his fists, leaving Colm to swing haplessly for all the digs he could lay into the collared one's belly and kidneys. Together they easily draged him further up the alley behind a row of industrial refuse bins. Erin followed at a steady pace, her pleasure increasing with every whack, smack, lick and punch. With all that force upon him, the collared one had no chance to inhale a decent bout of oxygen, let alone a scream for help. Puffing deeply, Erin felt her eyes fall into a fixated line of vision. She was wholly present in the enveloping scene laid out in front of her with no sense of danger, nor conscience. She cranked her neck, clicking once on each side. Eyes closed, she involuntarily invoked an image that immediately stirred her susceptibility to inimical rage...

Awaking in my bedroom to the blend of my mother's pleas for calm, I am reluctant to reach for the door, knowing the shrill will only become more piercing if I open it. Like any kid would, I do the exact opposite of what I know is good for me. "You think you can just come home from the football and the pub again in this state...and I'm going to put up with it and not bother my backside?" The jarred shrill becomes nullified only by my stepfather's stomping and drunken refusals. A crack of vinyl follows a short silence. Drums, flutes...The Sash My Father Wore. Full volume. All hell breaks loose and a cacophonous din rises through the floorboards as I hear my mother race across the lounge in pursuit of the record needle. The bouncing of tempers and the banging of furniture make me tense. I squirm. With a high-pitched scratch, the music stops abruptly. More banging follows towards the hallway door, as I half-heartedly prop myself up, only to hear words that I know will cause my gut to retch. With gritted teeth, I hear my mother. "I'm warning you...if you put that record, or any bloody record on again in this house, I'll..." "You'll what?" I hear my stepfather say like a world champion prick. I envisage him holding the record imperiously over the turntable. "I'M WARNING YOU..." she shouts. Without pause, my stepfather's voice is unrecognisable, full of venom. "Uch get up the stairs ya CATHOLIC CUNT!"

Instinctively, I lay face down away from the bedroom door, smothering my ears with a pillow...

Eyes open wide again, tunnelled and merciless and unrestrained, Erin scuttled through the strewn garbage. Her aim was her torment. With one swift, colossal swing of her right foot, her toe made direct contact with the collared one's neck.

Colm and Beamer stepped back, equally breathless and dripping with sweat. Erin pushed them away as she desired a moment to stand superiorly over her now prone antagonist. Bending down, she grabbed the collar, pulling the bloody face that wore it closer to her own.

"Get in another," Beamer blew.

"Yeah, give him a right deadly Glasgow kiss," Colm bounced.

Erin wasn't listening to either of them, their voices disappearing into an echoing vortex within the walls of the alley.

"NOW WHO'S THE FENIAN BITCH?" she roared with spit and gritted teeth. All the virulent memories she possessed coursed through every inch of her body.

She pushed the torso down, and obliged her accomplices with the fiercest Glasgow kiss her ire could generate. The force of it surprised her, causing the collared one's tracksuit top to tear in her hands, the zip disengaging itself down to the breastbone. She stood, dizzy with poignant exhilaration. Stumbling backwards, she was caught by Colm's arm.

Sandwiched between him and Beamer, Erin realised their whooping and hollering had ceased. She looked at them back and forth. Beamer's ashen face immediately disturbed her, remembering how, in their short acquaintance, his cheeks had never reduced paler than a lighter shade of ruddy. Erin noticed Colm holding the Zippo she must have dropped in the fray. Both pair of eyes bore through the stinking haze, but with distinctly different expressions from just minutes ago. Sighing with confusion, Erin looked down at the collar, its wearer spluttering in pain, writhing from side to side. Yet then, it wasn't solely the collar that was visible as the tracksuit top also lay open, exposing the blue, blood-stained shirt, its badge emblazoned with a gold cockerel perched on top of three Fs.

"À Thierry, avec toot mon amoor," Colm said randomly, quoting a meagre rendering of French.

"What the feck you on about?" Beamer blurted out. In the same moment as Beamer's *feck,* Erin realised Colm was reading an inscription engraved on the Zippo. She'd failed to notice it.

"He's not a feckin hun, this cunt," Colm bellowed. "He's a feckin FROG!"

With an intake of breath and an unintelligent squint of his eye, Beamer replied, "Well how the bejesus...? That French shirt looks exactly like the Rangers one."

"Except for the lack of *McEwan's Lager* printed across the front," Erin said calmly.

"Aye, that's some big feckin exception," Beamer croaked, one finger pointed at the Zippo, the other at the cockerel. "FUCK, COCK, FUCK!!!"

All Erin knew was that she didn't dare look under that collar. Her fear was...she might find a crucifix.

Cat Cochrane is a writer and journalist, published across local and national newspapers and magazines.

Sugartown is her first collection of short stories and poems. She lives in Glasgow's East End, where she is currently writing her second collection.

catcochrane_writer

Printed in Great Britain
by Amazon